Heat bloomed on her cheeks.

"You request these things as if I do not know the beauty spot beneath your left breast," Konstantinos continued, because he could not stop it. The words burning his throat dry. "As if I have not kissed it with my mouth—felt its texture with my tongue."

The tendons tightened in Poppy's throat. Her tongue crept out from the silken cocoon that housed it.

He watched the emotions flit across her face. The rise of heat bloom on her chest deepen the pinks on her already warm cheeks. The flare of her nostrils...

She was a liar.

He saw it. What she so desperately tried to conceal.

She wanted him. *Still.*

Lela May Wight grew up with seven brothers and sisters. Yes, it was noisy, and she often found escape in romance books. She still does, but now she gets to write them, too! She hopes to offer readers the same escapism when the world is a little too loud. Lela May lives in the UK with her two sons and her very own hero, who never complains about her book addiction—he buys her more books! Check out what she's up to at lelamaywight.com.

Books by Lela May Wight

Harlequin Presents

His Desert Bride by Demand
Bound by a Sicilian Secret
The King She Shouldn't Crave
Italian Wife Wanted
Kidnapped for Her Secret

Visit the Author Profile page at Harlequin.com.

BROKEN GREEK VOWS

LELA MAY WIGHT

PRESENTS

Harlequin® PRESENTS™

Recycling programs
for this product may
not exist in your area.

ISBN-13: 978-1-335-21394-5

Broken Greek Vows

Copyright © 2026 by Lela May Wight

Harlequin Enterprises ULC
22 Adelaide St. West, 41st Floor
Toronto, Ontario M5H 4E3, Canada
www.Harlequin.com

HarperCollins Publishers
Macken House, 39/40 Mayor Street Upper,
Dublin 1, D01 C9W8, Ireland
www.HarperCollins.com

Printed in Lithuania

1 2 3 4 5 6 7 8 9 10 LIT 28 27 26 25

BROKEN GREEK VOWS

For those who have lost,
and for those who still love.

PROLOGUE

Poppy Ariti spread the interlinking green stems holding violet purple, sunset orange and heaven's pink flower tips. She slotted them through the holes in the permanently placed vase.

Wildflowers. They were everywhere on the island, but these she'd picked for him.

'*Dors, mon petit,*' she sang, as she had on her every visit. A lullaby her mother had sung to her, and her grandmother to her mother. And now…

She sang it for her son.

She sang it for Isaak.

'Sleep, little one,' she said again, finishing her lullaby for the last time in a croaked gulp. She couldn't stop them. Could never stop them. Tears. They fell. But today she cried not only for him.

Poppy cried for herself.

Hot, slow tears of betrayal.

'Mrs Ariti, we have to go.'

Poppy turned to the shadow on her left, holding her small brown leather overnight bag. 'I know,' she said, because Serena was right. She understood her urgent tone was appropriate.

She swiped at her cheeks.

She wouldn't leave without saying goodbye.

Six months ago, she wouldn't have been able to contemplate leaving the Greek island of Sotiría. Her home. The one place she could be with him. *Isaak.* But she *had* to leave him. *Tonight.*

She could do this, she told herself.

She was…*better.*

'*Au revoir, bébé.*' She leaned forward and pressed her lips to the white stone and stood from her knelt position.

Serena took her elbow. 'Quickly now,' she said, pulling her into step beside her.

Hair lashed into Poppy's eyes. The coastal wind whipped at her cheeks, pushed her thick black woollen overcoat close to her breast, as if it tried to stop her escape.

Hurriedly, they made their way down the sloped path to the small boat waiting for them at the jetty. Serena, dressed all in black, stepped aboard first. She dropped Poppy's bag onto the decking, turned, and held out her gloved hand.

'Mind your step, Mrs Ariti.'

Poppy took her hand and placed her flat booted heel on the decking. She didn't correct her. She'd told Serena, her personal bodyguard since Konstantinos had slipped the engagement ring onto her finger three years ago, countless times to call her Poppy. And no longer was Poppy staff, but a soon-to-be tycoon's wife.

The paparazzi had swarmed.

She shuddered.

Formalities were unnecessary between them. Especially now Serena was no longer employed by her. In another life, she and Serena would have been friends, but not *this* one.

Poppy understood her need to keep the formal barrier between them.

She understood why, after the funeral, Serena had left her employment.

Isaak's death had hurt everyone. Everyone but *him. He'd* never got attached. Not to the idea of him. *Their son.* Whereas she…

She could almost feel Isaak. Here with her now, in her arms, holding him tightly to her chest as they escaped together into a new life. A life away from the man who had betrayed them both.

She closed her eyes. Tried to stem the pulsing ache in her stomach.

Konstantinos had never ached.

He'd never wanted a child, and neither had she, but their baby had been coming, yet still he hadn't wanted Isaak. He'd promised to do his duty. Fulfil his responsibility to the child. But that was where it ended.

Their relationship would remain as it was.

A marriage of convenience—friends with benefits—where he provided protection—*safety*—in return for her loyalty.

She hadn't craved a change in their marriage, but solidarity— *support*—for what was to come. A baby. *Their baby*. She'd needed her friend. *Him*. But instead of remaining friends and building a safe place for their child, they'd started to repel each other like opposing magnets.

They weren't friends now.

She opened her eyes.

'I'm sorry, Serena.' Guilt bloomed in her chest. 'I'm sorry I dragged you into all this.'

All those who lived in the monastery, the staff, they'd be crushed to learn their boss was a liar. *A cheat*. All of her husband's people were loyal to him. He inspired it. *Loyalty*. He was always fair to his employees. She couldn't trust anyone on the island not to tell him what she was doing—where she was going.

Serena wasn't crushed. She seemed almost relieved. Relieved that this man all believed was good was…*bad*. But still Poppy had put her in danger. Compromised her.

'It's such a risk to your reputation to help me,' she continued. 'A risk to your livelihood. I'm so thank—'

'Do *not* apologise for asking for help.' Serena's shoulders tensed into a straight line. 'Too many women ask for it too late. My mother…' Serena held her gaze in the shadows. 'I couldn't help *her* escape my father.'

Was it always the fathers who broke their little girls? Fathers who put the responsibility of protecting their mothers on their too-small shoulders?

You didn't protect her.

Her breath hitched.

She'd tried.

Too late.

The crash had taken her mother and father before she could. And *that* would always be her burden to carry. Yes, she'd been a child, but it was her regret to own. And she owned it as hers. Even if the lie belonged to her father.

'My father…he hurt my mother, too. Lied to her.' An ugly curve tilted her lips. '*Men*…they can't be trusted. They're all liars.'

It had been her mantra all of her life. Never to trust them, however charming they were, like her dad.

Konstantinos had changed her mind.

She'd been a fool to believe she could trust him. She'd thought he was different. *Special.*

Konstantinos Ariti had fooled everyone. He hadn't been giving her time, not when Isaak was growing inside her, and not when he was gone. He hadn't kept his distance to give her time to heal. To get better.

He'd been having an affair.

The private investigator recommended to her by Serena had confirmed her suspicions.

He'd betrayed her at her most vulnerable.

He was never the man she'd thought he was.

He was a liar.

She looked up at the converted monastery on the hill. If she'd kept her barriers high, if she hadn't let him in, if she'd kept their relationship formal—kept it employee and employer—if she'd never kissed him on their first overseas work trip together…

In London everything had changed. She'd abandoned the fight with herself and admitted what she felt was more than admiration.

She wanted him.

He'd leaned in and held her so close, and yet so far.

She'd always wanted to kiss him. To feel his mouth on hers, and trace the shape of it with her tongue—*learn it*. She'd devoted her eyes to his lips in every minute she'd sat in a boardroom with her ex-boss watching them. His lips. This mouth that spoke words of truth. *Honesty*. So strong was his conviction that he had to protect everyone. His employees. *His people*, as he called them, promising he'd keep them safe from the monsters at their doors. Protect their mental health.

She'd leaned in all the way.

She had kissed him.

He'd stopped her. Told her if this happened, what it would be. An affair, but he'd never ask for more than what she wanted to give and he'd expect the same from her. If they did this, he'd adore her body and her mind, he'd protect them both, but he'd never love her.

Poppy hadn't wanted love—never again would she chase a feeling.

She'd believed he was the one man she could trust, because everything he did was with brutal honesty. She'd thought she was safe with him. Safe from lies, even the ones that hurt, because he'd always promised to be honest with her. She'd felt safe enough to be honest with him. To tell him what she wanted. *Needed*.

Always honesty. Always the truth.

He'd agreed, and she'd answered with her mouth. Her tongue.

His honesty had made her feel safe, safe enough to take the risk of trusting him.

But she'd had to find *this* out on her own. The truth.

They'd never been friends.

She'd never been anything more to him than what *he* needed.

A wife to strengthen his image and bolster his reputation of being a family-led business. Their marriage in public and behind closed doors…it was all a façade, because the man beneath his perfect image was a *cheat*.

She closed her eyes briefly. She wouldn't wish *they* had never happened. Because if they hadn't, she would never have got pregnant. She never would have held him. Her baby boy.

Asleep, he'd been so very beautiful. *So perfect*.

Poppy closed her mouth too late to contain the muffled sob.

She knew it wasn't her fault. After months of therapy, she understood it was no one's fault. She understood the logic of this truth. The physics of placental abruption. The part of her body meant to nourish him had started to detach. The abruption only minor at first, the doctors had put her on bedrest. Guarded by nurses. But it hadn't been enough. Isaak had been born sleeping.

She understood future pregnancies wouldn't be the same.

Her throat closed.

Logic didn't cushion the pain. Nor did biology.

Serena held out a life jacket. 'Let's put this on.'

Poppy nodded and let Serena direct her limbs inside the vest. She pulled the last buckle tight.

'Did you do as I said?' she asked.

'No credit cards. Only—' her chest tightened '—*cash*.'

She didn't have nearly enough.

Serena nodded. 'Sit down, and hold on.'

She sat down on the wooden bench beside her. Serena brought the engine to life. It purred, its revs hidden by the roll of the waves of the Ionian Sea aiding their escape.

The boat sliced through the water, which shone in the headlights like a trail of rippling diamonds guiding them directly towards the mouth of the island.

The only way in.

The only way *out*.

'It's time to drop your phone over the side,' she said, keeping her hands on the silver steering wheel and her eyes straight ahead. 'He'll track it if you don't.'

If he found her trying to leave, he'd never let her go.

Divorce. He didn't believe in it. A divorce was a broken promise. He didn't break his. He wouldn't let her forget hers. His image was everything. Their marriage had been negotiated to last forever. Two people who could rely on each other. A loveless match bound by the things she wanted—trust and respect—and in exchange he would have what he wanted too. Their marriage would make his image complete. His reputation the opposite of his father's brutal empire.

All a lie.

All a front for the public.

He'd broken the promises that meant the most to her. To always be honest. Faithful. *Loyal.* Her heart ached behind her breastbone. He knew about her dad. His adultery. He'd promised never—

Her heart squeezed.

Had he been having an affair while she was on bedrest? While her body had been nurturing their son?

Acrid acid burnt its way up her throat.

She looked at her rings.

She should drop those in, too.

She slipped them off, and pocketed them. She'd sell them when she got to France. Her homeland. She knew no one waited for her there. All her family was gone.

She swallowed. Her old employer would understand her grief. Her need for refuge. A place to hide until she was… *strong.* Strong enough to fight him for a divorce. She tensed. The idea of *that* confrontation now… His betrayal… His abandonment. Her nose pinched.

She couldn't.

'Okay.' Poppy pulled her phone out of her pocket. She'd kept it so they could communicate. Serena had made her download some encrypted app two weeks ago when she'd called her about arranging a PI. They'd messaged on it today with details of their plan. It was all happening so quickly…

She inhaled a stuttering breath.

She entered the pin.

The screen was illuminated.

She hadn't closed it. The message. The attachment was still there. Still open. It wouldn't matter if she closed it. Her phone was set to upload to the cloud. Making it forever available.

A photograph of her husband.

His mouth locked on another's.

'How long until we get to the plane?' Poppy asked tightly.

'My team are all set and waiting on a deserted island not too far from here.' Her gaze dropped to her wrist. She lifted it. A green light shone beneath the cuff. 'Twenty minutes.'

She looked back at the converted monastery, alight at the top of the cliff. The monks had lived here long ago. It was the place she'd called home for the last three years. A home he'd converted just for them. A place she'd thought was her forever home.

'Don't worry,' Serena said, drawing Poppy's gaze. 'I'll get you into France without your arrival being official. He'll never know where you went. You'll just…*vanish*.' She made short, firm eye contact. 'It'll be as if you never existed.'

That's what *he* wanted, wasn't it?

He was having an affair to avoid the tragedy their marriage had become by pretending his wife and son didn't exist.

A tear slipped free.

She didn't know if she'd ever be ready to confront *that*. Or him.

She exhaled slowly through her nostrils.

Maybe she would never have to.

Maybe *this* was the end of it.

The end of *them*.

She stretched her arm over the side of the boat. She held it there. Her fingers trembled.

'Goodbye, Konstantinos.'

She let go of her phone. Into the water's dark depths it disappeared.

And so, too, did Poppy.

CHAPTER ONE

Twelve Months Later...

Poppy pushed up the sash window. The air was too stifling. *Too close*, her mother would have said. As if the air itself was closing in.

It was a warning the storm was near.

Soon the heavens would open.

The sky would tear with lightning bolts.

The thunder would roar.

But outside, there were no signs of an incoming storm. All was as it had been for the last year. *Picturesque.* Not a cloud was in the sky. The sun shone over Paris in a blanket of warm orange. The Champ de Mars was a forest of green beneath the Eiffel Tower. A postcard picture she only viewed from inside. Hidden behind the glass. Safe inside her temporary home.

She'd always known it would be temporary. Yet she wasn't ready to leave. She wasn't ready to face the world outside the haven this place had become to her. A place to heal.

She exhaled sharply.

She knew the closeness of the storm wasn't making her skin clammy, though. It was the telephone meeting taking place a few rooms down.

'I'm so sorry, my dear.'

Léon Durand. Her old employer had opened his home to her

without condition, but with empathy. They'd both lost so much. They'd…*talked*. Of their losses. Of hers.

Léon was a blessing. He always had been. Her very first employer straight out of university. Durand Cruise Liners never should have hired her. She'd been too inexperienced, despite her double degrees and her aptitude for languages, to be a personal assistant to the head of a conglomerate. But it was an unusual position no experienced PA would have agreed to.

His son, Caleb, had taken over the family business. Léon's position within his own company had become redundant, his staff had been reduced or transferred, and yet he stayed in his office. He refused to officially retire. Caleb had confided he did this because no one was at home any more. His wife had died. He was alone in a six-storey mansion. And so he stayed in his second home. Durand Towers. Poppy was hired to keep Léon…*company*. A companion.

And now they were each other's.

'There's nothing I can do,' Léon said quietly from the doorway. 'There's no way to stop it.'

Her mouth ran dry.

'The lawyers have delayed as much as they can, but they have come to the end of the road. There are no more loopholes to use.' He swallowed thickly. 'The takeover is imminent.'

She nodded, and turned her gaze away from where he sat in his wheelchair.

Guilt pressed down heavily on her heart.

She never should have put Léon in this position, but she hadn't known about the loan. Hadn't known how close the spider was coming to wrapping its silken threads around Léon.

She picked up her pruning shears. She'd spent the last year honing in on the things she enjoyed. Flowers. Arranging them into subtle bouquets—large ones, fantastical ones. Léon's home looked somewhat like a florist's shop now. But they both enjoyed the scent. The scent of hope the greyness of grief would dim.

'Use *this* as an opportunity, Poppy,' Léon said behind her. 'Face him.'

The pruning shears slipped from her fingers onto the mat-lined table. White petals fell from the long-stemmed roses she was arranging in the vase with the thud of metal on wood.

She shook her head. 'I can't.'

'You must at least talk—'

'I don't want to talk to him,' she interjected sharply. *Too sharply.*

'If only to end it,' he pressed. 'Divorce him.'

She closed her eyes. Shut out the view of Paris in front of her. Shut out the voice of reason behind her.

'You can't hide forever.'

She sighed. 'I'm not ready.'

'We are never ready for these things.'

Poppy opened her eyes. For a year, she'd waited for it. For strength. But she wasn't…*strong.*

She fingered a thornless stem with her left hand. A year later and still it felt wrong not to be wearing her rings. Her hand—her fingers—they were unbalanced without them.

'We both know you can't continue to live like this,' he said, rolling his wheelchair beside her. 'You cannot live with me as you have done. As if the world outside doesn't exist. *It* exists, Poppy, and it's coming inside. *He* is.'

A tremble raked through her. 'How long do I have?'

'A week. *Maybe.*' He reached for her hand. Enclosed it between both of his. Such a simple gesture of reassurance that he was here. With her. Her friend. 'I'm in no position to delay him.'

She looked down into his weathered face. He looked so much older than he had when she'd met him almost a decade ago. She recognised the deeper lines. She had them too. Scars of sadness. *Grief.* Both had aged him ten years above his seventy. As for her…she didn't feel thirty. She ached in places no thirty-year-old should.

Her eyes welled. 'You shouldn't have to,' she said, placing her free hand on top of his. 'I never meant to stay this long.'

His face twisted. '*I* was selfish to keep you here. Selfish not to push you to do *this* sooner. But you—your memories of Caleb—' His voice broke.

Her throat clogged. Poppy had worked for the Durands for twelve months before Léon retired. Then she'd become Caleb's *third* assistant. Caleb had never been anything more to her than an employer, although she had seen his determination to keep the business and his family from bankruptcy. But by her fourth year working for the family the business had come under real strain, despite his best efforts, and he started letting staff go...

She never should have taken Konstantinos's job offer.

But she had. Konstantinos had seen in her something no one else ever had. The potential to be...*more*. Potential he'd highlighted in a meeting when she'd suggested a workable time-line so Konstantinos and Caleb could work together to ease the worries of a cargo business they'd intended to take over, *together*, to minimise the monetary risk to their individual businesses. Especially as Durand was looking into new ventures to stabilise the company's income.

He'd told them a young woman brave enough to speak out in a meeting where she should be taking minutes needed to be given the opportunity to grow. There was no room for professional growth in a business that was letting staff go, closing departments and taking risks on new ventures.

Konstantinos hadn't stolen her away. He wasn't underhand. He'd asked them if he could have her. They'd agreed to let her go.

She'd become PA to the richest shipping magnate in the world. Konstantinos had given her an opportunity no one else had, an opportunity to grow, to be more, but still her eyes had chased his lips into every room—watched them until London.

He'd pushed her in the office to take charge of her professional growth, and every chance they had he pushed her in bed too—to demand more. To tell him what she liked when he kissed the skin beneath her ear. When he put his hand between her thighs.

He'd made her feel free to be honest, when all her young life she'd held her tongue, considered the consequences of her honesty.

She didn't have to consider the consequences with *him*.

He'd become her lover. Her friend. She'd told him things she'd told no one. Her father was an adulterer. She'd spent her childhood holding her breath.

He'd promised she'd never have to hold her breath with him.

She never had to be scared.

When he'd asked her to marry him…it had been the happily-ever-after she wanted. Not love, but friendship. *Trust*.

'Caleb was a good man,' she said, pushing *those* memories of Konstantinos down.

Konstantinos wasn't the man he made people believe he was. He wasn't trustworthy. He wasn't on her side. He'd left her side the minute the pregnancy test had shown two vivid pink lines. He'd abandoned her completely when she was grieving. *Sick*.

Postpartum depression. What a cruel thing for her body to do to her. To give her all the emotions of a woman who'd carried her baby into the third trimester, twenty-eight weeks, and amplify them with grief.

'And a terrible businessman,' Léon said.

She dropped her stiff shoulders. None of this was Léon's fault. He'd given her refuge. He'd done everything in his power to hide her in plain sight.

'We can't all be good at everything,' she soothed.

He smiled, but it didn't reach his eyes. 'I should have held on to the reins a little longer,' he said. 'I should have—'

'You did nothing wrong, Léon.'

'If I'd done things differently…if I hadn't retired…' His lips thinned. 'Your husband would never have had to bail us out. Save my company from bankruptcy. *You* wouldn't be in the position you are in now.'

'No one put me in this position but *him*.'

She'd thought she was safe with Konstantinos.

'You came when I had nothing and no one.' Léon's eyes shimmered.

'I had no one either,' she said.

'You *have* a husband,' he corrected.

'He stopped being *that* the minute he was unfaithful.' Fury burned beneath her skin. 'He betrayed *me*.'

Léon scowled. 'I'm sorry, Poppy. Sorry I didn't push you to at least end it. Close the door on your marriage before it came to this point. *Critical*.'

'You gave me what I needed,' she corrected. 'A friend.'

'Our time is up.' He paled. 'He *will* take over Durand's. He will come.'

'I'll leave.'

'I have an estate.' He frowned. 'It is rural. Deep in the countryside. It's yours, if this is what you wish.'

She leant down and kissed his cheek. 'Thank you.'

He nodded. 'I'll do everything in my power to give you what you…*need*.'

Twenty-four hours later…

Konstantinos Ariti was no saviour.

He was the devil.

And tonight he'd come to collect.

He rang the gold bell, and within seconds the black iron doors of the six-storey French mansion in the seventh arrondissement of Paris opened.

It was a unique property with generations' worth of history engraved into the high gold-leaf ceilings, into the ornate cornices of the Haussmann architecture and buried deep into the herringbone floors.

'This way, sir.'

He strode inside and swept past the straight spine and the dipped head of the butler without greeting. He knew the way, but he also knew who he'd find inside the formal dining room when he arrived… Léon was changed.

It wouldn't be the same as their meeting three years ago. Laughter wouldn't be heard above clinking glasses.

His Adam's apple dragged heavily up and down his throat.

He didn't let his eyes linger on the portraits of those loved and lost lining the walls, but a stillness only attributed to the forever sleeping, and those they left behind wide awake, hung in the air like a sickness.

On leather-cushioned feet, he entered another corridor.

His gaze stalled on the adaptations not in keeping with the décor. The stairlift, customised to encircle the spiralling stair-case. The solid wooden ramp leading up the short three steps to a closed door.

Another bowed head greeted him at the end of the corridor. A white-gloved hand pressed down the gold handle to open an ornate door expanded to allow for a wider gait.

He stepped inside.

The panelled windows, the palest of pinewood adorned with ornate gold rims, let in the view and the orange light of a setting sun over the heart of Paris. Clear vases full of white blooms with overly long green stems adorned every polished surface. The chandelier roared with the tiny flames of dozens of thin church candles above the table. An oval top made of rosewood, dressed with silver cutlery, and crystal glasses, held the central piece. A bigger vase held longer stems, bigger blooms.

The smell of death didn't live here.

It was floral.

It was Poppy.

His wife.

He clenched his teeth.

She was everywhere and nowhere.

The ghost of her had walked beside him on every street for a year. She'd sat beside him—*distracted him*—in every meeting, on every plane ride across the ocean to see for himself if his team had the right woman this time. If they'd found her. And each time, it hadn't been her.

She'd simply stopped existing. And yet, she was in the very air he breathed.

He squeezed the bridge of his nose between his thumb and forefinger.

He'd thought they were the same. Level-headed.

He'd never wanted to marry. He'd thought his actions would be enough to prove to the world he was nothing like his father, but when the articles had turned into a frenzy after his award for providing a work-life balance for his employees and their families, the mock outrage that he had no family, that *he* wasn't married… It became front-page news.

He'd known there was one way to end the speculation he was anything like his tyrant of a father.

He'd known he could do it with Poppy. A marriage of convenience. A marriage based on sex, but in public they'd be the epitome of a healthy relationship. Childless, but still whole. A couple who respected each other.

His father had never respected his mother, but *he* had respected Poppy. Respected her boundaries set into place because of her childhood. As she respected his.

Never emotion.

Never love.

She'd wanted only the things he could give her.

The things *she* wanted.

Security—*loyalty*—sex.

He'd given her all three in exchange for a marriage of convenience to bolster the image of his business ethos. *Family and health first.*

The press had torn him apart with her disappearance. The image of her on the cliff. The stolen photograph of his wife in despair. *Lost.* Displayed for the world to see. Captioned in sensational, vulgar words in gossip and news columns worldwide accusing *him* of hiding her away because of his advocacy for mental health, and how badly it would look if he couldn't support his wife.

It wasn't true.

He'd made sure she had everything his mother hadn't. *Help.*

He walked further into the room, empty but for the sound of his breath leaving his flaring nostrils.

'Konstantinos,' a voice called from the doorway.

He turned, and his instinct was to let his gaze linger on the wheelchair, on the legs, smaller now, outlined beneath the grey wool blanket keeping them warm. But he didn't. He made himself look straight into the eyes of the cruise-liner tycoon, and swallowed down the words of condolence in his throat.

He wouldn't let himself care for anything or anyone any more.

He'd cared for *her*, and she'd betrayed him. He'd trusted her to keep her word.

No one would leave him behind again.

Tonight, he'd let himself be everything he'd fought against becoming all his life. His father.

He'd be brutal. Ruthless. *Cruel.*

He'd make himself enjoy this, because what was the alternative?

It was his reputation or the cruise-liner tycoon's.

It wasn't personal.

This was business.

The only personal connection they'd ever had was *her*. Their meeting three years ago should never have been what it was.

A date. It had gone from formal to casual when *she'd* joined them, not as anyone's employee, but as his wife. Caleb's wife had joined them too, at Poppy's request. And she'd joined them with their daughter in tow, who'd fallen asleep before dessert on her grandfather's knee. Against Léon's chest.

He snarled.

He was a fool.

He'd known the Durands most of his life. He'd been to boarding school with the tycoon's son. But they were not friends.

Poppy was your friend.

He stepped forward.

She was nothing to him now.

He stretched out his hand. 'Léon,' he greeted in return without inflection.

'Konstantinos,' he repeated, wrapping two hands around his. 'Thank you for coming so quickly.'

'I was already in Paris.'

He released his hand. 'I was aware.'

Konstantinos stood tall and watched him roll his wheelchair into place at the head of the table.

Léon nodded to the chair beside him. 'Sit with me.'

Konstantinos exhaled. One foot after the other, he took his seat beside him at a table Konstantinos had shared with him and his family three years ago when he'd saved the tycoon's business by pumping millions into it.

He never should have given them the loan. The business had been failing. *Rapidly.* It was high-risk. A risk he wouldn't usually take. But the dinner…when the two wives had put the little girl to bed. Leaving the men downstairs to talk. To keep business and family separate. It had done something to him. Seduced him with its family foundations.

He'd never had a conventional family. But he'd known *that* night, watching them all, why he did what he did. Why when his mother had died, he'd sworn to be the opposite of his father, and build an empire that put family and health first.

Family—it gave them each strength. A strength his mother had been denied by his father.

His entire business model was about putting family first. A vow he'd promised to his mother when he'd held her in his arms. He'd promised he'd prove it didn't have to be the way it was for her.

No one had to be put second place to money. Or power. *No one.*

It had felt like a moral obligation to save them all.

And he had.

He'd saved Léon's family business *that* night.

But now Léon had no family.

And neither did he.

Now… Konstantinos would protect only himself.

Konstantinos eyed the perfectly set table. The three crystal goblets. 'Why are there three place settings?' he asked.

'I thought tonight might call for a mediator,' Léon admitted.

He frowned. 'A mediator?'

'I expect there will be difficult discussions.' His loosened skin rolled with the heavy drag of his Adam's apple. 'About your wife.'

'My wife is none of your business,' he warned.

'Of course she's my business. *She* is why you're here. You have come to deflect the salacious rumours: *"Is she in the attic?"'* he pressed, repeating the recent headlines. '*"Has Konstantinos lost his business acumen and his wife?"'*

Intelligent blue eyes met his. They were still sharp, yet they were glazed—*fogged*—by too many defeats.

'The rumours won't end because you take over *my* organisation,' Léon finished.

'They will,' Konstantinos countered.

He'd show them all he was stronger than he'd ever been. Before or after *her*.

'They won't. The press—' Léon's nostrils flared '—they question my mental health with their disgusting articles, because I sought refuge in my home after the death of my family.' He continued, 'And they mock *you* because of the disappearance of your wife after losing your son. They parade our grief daily.'

His throat dried. Images, too bright—*too clear*—burst to vivid clarity in his mind.

His son in his arms.

The weightlessness of him.

His ears had strained to hear the whoosh of a heart that no longer beat. To hear his son breathe. He'd placed his too big hand to his still chest. Waited for his eyes to open. But they hadn't. His eyes had never opened. So peaceful he had looked.

You failed him.

He hadn't kept his promise. He hadn't protected them when he'd vowed he would. Protected them both from the monster that lived inside him. A monster like his father who could abandon all those he should have protected.

He'd never wanted to risk having a child.

He'd wanted his father's DNA to stop with him.

And it had.

Isaak was dead, because *he'd* willed it.

He stiffened. Tentacles of grief wrapped around his vital organs and squeezed.

Konstantinos cut them down at the root.

He refused to allow anything like what he'd experienced after his mother's death to enter his bloodstream ever again.

He wouldn't grieve for someone who had never lived.

He wouldn't think of him.

His son. Born too soon…

'Let them whisper, Konstantinos,' Léon urged. 'These men who watched you grow into a man and build a shipping empire bigger than your father's—they have turned their backs on us both.' His lips pursed. 'So let them take their business deals elsewhere. Let it all fall to the bottom of the sea. None of it matters.'

The rumours were true.

Léon *had* given up.

'You're ready to lose everything?' His gaze narrowed. '*To me?*'

'Everything that mattered has already been taken from me,' he dismissed with a wave of his too thin wrist.

Konstantinos recoiled. His acceptance was an ugly thing. Léon was dead already. He'd died two years ago when they'd pulled the only survivor from the helicopter crash. *Him.* His son, his daughter-in-law and his granddaughter, gone.

Like Isaak?

He grimaced. He wouldn't form a connection between them because of their losses. This was business. Nothing else.

His father had been right all along. Power only remained with those willing to take it—with those who would do *anything* to keep it.

Konstantinos's chair scraped against the floor as he stood. 'As of tonight, Durand Cruise Liners belongs to me to settle the debt you owe me.'

'As is your right,' Léon agreed flatly.

He closed his eyes.

It was relief, not doubt, making his skin…*uncomfortable.* He was shedding a suit he'd resewn too many times to count to fit a man he'd thought was fair, but a man he now knew was a fool. But he'd corrected his error in judgement. He'd sliced off all of his soft edges with the blade that had cut free months of hair he'd let grow too thick, and too long, looking for a wife who didn't want to be found.

What if she's still sick?

The image of her on the clifftop drifted into his mind.

His jaw firmed to granite.

She'd made her choice, and now…

He'd made his.

He opened his eyes. 'The papers will arrive tomorrow,' he said. '*You* will sign them.'

Léon dipped his head. 'I will.'

It didn't feel like victory.

It felt like…*nothing*.

Konstantinos turned to leave…

A coldness expanded in his core, turning the blood in his body into a thick and sluggish pulp. It moved through his limbs at a glacial pace—refusing to pump into the heart now beating too slowly in his ears.

He swayed on his feet.

In slow motion, his gaze moved over the face in the doorway, watching him with blue eyes framed by obscenely long lashes, making them appear bigger—*deeper*. So similar to the eyes he'd searched for in every crowd these past twelve months.

His lungs forgot to inhale.

His unblinking gaze moved over her diamond-shaped face, her high cheekbones flushed with freckles, her flicked nose, her haunting rose-pink mouth wide and gaping. Her hair was loose. Longer now, skirting the open collar of her too big, long-sleeved white shirt. It came to her blue denim-clad thighs…

He took a step back on stiff knees.

It couldn't be.

'You…you…betrayed me,' she said brokenly. Her eyes no longer on his, but on…

He blinked. *Slowly.* He followed her gaze.

'Forgive me, Poppy,' Léon pleaded. 'You will see—*in time*—it was the right choice to bring your husband here tonight. The *only* choice. I'm sorry I didn't warn you. I knew you'd flee…' Léon's voice spoke softly beside him. 'But I will stay here with *you. If* you want me to.'

Konstantinos's mind whirled.

Léon was the mediator?

He turned his gaze back to her.

His wife.

For a year, Konstantinos had searched. The night terrors had returned. Crashing waves and seaweed. But it hadn't been his mother he'd fought against the current to save. It had been *Poppy*, caught in the green weeds of the sea. *Drowning*.

Flashlights on the heads of the specialist teams searching the island's waters, the whoosh of the helicopters swarming over the hills, and the cliffs, trying to find her the night she'd vanished, pummelled his mind's eye.

She was the one he'd vowed to keep safe. He hadn't been able to keep his mother safe. He hadn't protected her from the monsters in her head or the real live monster—his father—who had berated her for being sick.

His father had abandoned his mother.

He…he hadn't abandoned Poppy. Not when she was physically sick, not when her mental health had failed her. *He'd* protected Poppy. *He* was not his father. But *she* had walked away anyway.

Abandoned him.

Just like your mother?

His chest squeezed.

You failed your mother.

You failed Poppy.

You let your son die.

You failed them all.

The breath in his throat turned heavy—threatening to choke him.

He'd done everything right to keep them safe.

He wasn't at fault.

She was.

She'd destroyed everything he'd built.

She'd destroyed *him*.

Heat flushed through his body. The ice in his veins shattered, replaced by a roaring inferno.

She'd promised she would always be there, by his side, and she…betrayed him.

And Léon, after everything he'd done for him and his family, had harboured his runaway wife. Hidden her from *him*.

Great lava waves crashed against his chest wall.

'For all this time?' Konstantinos's feet moved of their own volition towards her motionless frame in the doorway. 'You've been…*here*?'

Her eyes bulged. She stepped back on flat black pumps, and raised her arms, outstretched them, palms forward, as if to ward him off.

Her eyes moved to the corridor beyond the room in front of her.

'Popp—'

She turned her feet in the direction of her eyes. She moved. Her pumps squeaked.

He leapt into motion. Any heaviness in his core evaporated. His adrenaline spiked, giving life to his limbs. His brisk step covering more than her run, he followed her back the way he'd come.

She stopped at the entrance—reached for the handles.

She looked up.

Their gazes locked.

It pulsed between them. A vortex of all that was unsaid. *So many questions*. His neck corded, and he choked down every single one in his throat, and said, 'Come to me.'

She dragged her gaze back to the oak and iron trapping her inside.

'Do not open those doors,' he warned.

Her fingers flexed on the handles.

His solar plexus tightened.

She yanked open the doors.

It ripped through him. *Rage.*

Strawberry blonde wisps of hair flying in all directions, she disappeared through the open doors. *Out of sight.*

A guttural roar built in his chest.

Konstantinos moved to the entrance, and he howled into the Parisian night.

'*Poppy!*'

CHAPTER TWO

Poppy understood it for what it was.

A battle cry.

Rough and accented, the roar of her name swept over her skin and called every hair on her body to rise to it.

For months she'd hidden from this fight, and she didn't want it. She wasn't ready.

Eyes forward, she ran. Her feet faltered with the hiccup of her heart. But she wouldn't stop. She wouldn't turn back.

She wasn't stupid. At her fastest, she couldn't match his stealth. She couldn't outpace him. But she *could* hide.

Ahead, the unmarked border between the seventh and fifteenth districts called to her.

She ran beneath a broken streetlight and slipped into the alley between two tall buildings.

She scanned what loomed above her on either side. Apartments. Metal balconies covered each wall with a crisscross of diagonal steps. A pull-down ladder hovered above her. *A fire escape?*

She jumped— missing the first rung by too many centimetres.

She scanned the lower walls—the white doors. She tugged at a silver handle. *Locked.*

She turned her gaze to the end of the alleyway.

Her heart stopped.

Metal gates barred her way. She ran to them. Yanked at the

padlock. *Futile*. Her gaze lifted. Her stomach dropped. She couldn't climb the twisted metal with its sharp, dagger points.

'Poppy,' a voice said behind her. It was quiet. *Lethal*.

Her heart slowed. Her panting lungs ceased to breathe.

She whipped around.

His frame filled the entrance to the alleyway. Blocked any chance of escape. Dressed all in black, he was an all-consuming shadow in the darkness.

And he was getting closer.

'*Ahh!*' A noise left her mouth that should have been a scream, but it wasn't. It was a yip that sounded too much like excitement. As if it wanted to be caught, and it enjoyed the thrill of the chase.

Her body was confused. It was too tightly coiled. *Too tense. It was not excited!*

She hated confrontation—had hidden from it since she was a child for fear of exposing her father's double life. She'd run tonight because it was instinct to run. The way it had been when she'd been young. Run away from the lies her father told her mother. The heated arguments that followed. But…

She swallowed. *Hard*. But there was no moisture to smooth the motion. No way to ease the tightness drawing her every muscle taut. But never had the threat of confrontation felt so… *internal*.

It was bone-deep. It throbbed in her temples, in her chest. And down lower. Between her thighs.

His step didn't falter. Graceful and slow, he closed the distance between them with effortless ease.

The amber light from the windows up on high threw a light down on him—sharpened his edges.

His black hair was scraped back with precision. Each strand in place. *Perfect*. His broad forehead drew her gaze to his eagle nose, his clean-shaven sculpted cheekbones, his thick, naturally pouting mouth. The open collar of his black shirt exposed his wide neck, taut and pulsing. His black suit, his jacket unbuttoned, sat on his shoulders like a second skin.

He was everything she remembered, and everything she'd tried to forget.

A beautiful liar.

He stopped in front of her.

'You will come with me.' He raised long, tanned fingers.

Was he trembling?

No.

Konstantinos didn't tremble.

He felt nothing.

She stepped back out of reach. Her back met metal. 'Don't touch me.'

She didn't want his hands on her.

She didn't crave his touch.

She didn't miss the sweep of his fingers on her skin.

She didn't yearn for the all-encompassing heat of his body enveloping her.

She didn't long for the security of his arms.

He wasn't safe.

His gaze narrowed. 'Don't touch you?'

Her stomach flipped. 'Go away, Konstantinos.'

He inched towards her. Invaded her space. Swallowed the air and replaced it with him. *Only him.* And it washed over her. A scent so familiar, so earthy.

She wouldn't breathe him in!

But she already had. *Too deeply.* All she could taste was him. And he tasted of the shattered shards of broken vows.

'I'm going nowhere without you.'

'Why would I go anywhere with you?'

Dark eyes burrowed into hers. 'You abandoned me—imploded my life. Devastated my reputation,' he said on a heated hiss. 'You owe me an explanation.'

She wouldn't feel guilty.

He deserved it!

He was a fraud.

Just like Dad.

'I owe you nothing.'

'Oh, but you do, *poulaki mou*.'

The endearment thrust her back to too long ago, to a once-upon-a-time fairy tale that had never existed.

'I'm *not* your little bird.' She spat out the lie, because she had been his. *Only his*.

The mighty Konstantinos Ariti had given her a chance to be…*more*. He'd said she was like a little bird tapping on the window when she'd spoken in *that* meeting. And he'd opened it.

It had done something to her. Stroked a part of her she'd thought she'd buried. The need to be chosen. Her dad had never chosen her. He'd never given up his other family. But Konstantinos had chosen *her*.

Each stage of their relationship, he'd sucked her in. Offered her a job no one else believed she could do. First assistant. A personal assistant to a formidable Greek. He'd eased her into a twelve-month affair. Tempted her into marriage. And for eighteen months before she fell pregnant it had been everything he'd promised.

He'd made her believe for the first time in her life she was safe. She could trust in the life she was living. The life she'd chosen to live with *him*.

He'd made her believe *he* could be trusted.

And then… *Isaak*.

He'd changed everything. Changed her. But Konstantinos had shown his true colours. He was cold. *Detached*. He'd never cared for her. Never cared for the baby they'd made. And she… she had cared. *Deeply*. So very deeply had she cared for them both, she realised.

She'd broken no rules. She had *not* fallen in love. But caring?

She'd carried his child. Wasn't she supposed to care?

Wasn't he?

'No,' he agreed. 'You're not a little bird any more.'

His gaze travelled over her. His slow appraisal, the flick of too long eyelashes, swept over every part of her body.

It was too intimate. It licked at her flesh. Made her burn.

Lean, long fingers rose to her cheek. Feather-light, his thumb grazed her cheek and pushed the stray hairs behind her ear. 'You are my wife.'

Electrical currents zapped her senses. The possessive statement, the imprint of his thumb on her over-sensitised skin, hardened her abdominal muscles. Her breasts felt heavy. The tight tips of her nipples pushed against the cotton of her shirt.

Whatever was happening inside her body was nothing more than muscle memory. Her body remembered, that was all. But his hands on her body. His touch on her skin…

It repulsed her, she assured herself.

He did *not* set her soul on fire.

The coil inside her, *suppressing everything*, popped.

'Get your hands off me.' Red rage misted her gaze. Never again would she welcome his touch on her body. *'You…you lying bastard!'*

His hand fell to his side. 'I have never lied to you.'

Did he really think she didn't know?

The heat drained from her limbs—blanching her tightened cheeks.

He knew what he'd done. He knew, even if she'd never confronted him with the photographs. He was there. He didn't need to see them.

Images of skin, dark and flawless, so different from her freckled, pale skin, flashed in her mind.

Isabella, she'd like her. Hired her as her replacement. She'd trained her.

The roll of tyres burst the tension between them.

Her gaze flicked to the black limousine blocking the entry to the alley.

'You will come with me,' he said again.

She thrust out her chin defiantly. 'I won't.'

'I have searched the world to find you. I thought you were dead, but here you are, very much alive.' His black eyes shot flames. '*This* doesn't end with me leaving you all alone in the dark.'

She needed this to end.

Them to end.

So, what choice did she have?

She hadn't been trying to heal these last months.

She'd been hiding. All her life she'd hidden from the moments she shouldn't have. The moments she should have stiffened her spine and planted her feet and spoken. However nasty it was to tell it. To say it out loud. The truth.

Léon was right. Right to make her face him. She needed to. But…

Her stomach dropped.

How many times had she run from confrontation? Away from her father? Hidden under the bed when she was too young to leave the house? Hidden in the park when she knew that was the furthest she could go on their estate? She'd never confronted him. Never told her mother the truth…

Poppy understood she hadn't kept her father's secrets only to protect her mother. She'd kept them to protect herself. To keep her father where he belonged. *With her.*

She'd wanted her daddy. *His love.*

What ten-year-old didn't?

It wasn't a special kind of love. He wasn't a special man. He had no admirable qualities other than that he was there. So many of the children at school…their families were broken. *Divorced.* They'd teased her because she was the odd one out with her traditional family. *Two parents*. They'd warned her it wouldn't last. Her daddy would leave. Just as their daddies had left them.

For so long she had thought her daddy wasn't like other daddies.

She'd joined the dots in her teens. They weren't simply *other children* she played with in the park on her Saturday afternoons out with her father. They were her family. Her half-siblings. Her father had a second family.

She'd wanted to tell her mother. Tell her the truth. Her father was splitting his time between two lives. Both a secret from the other. But she'd been afraid. Afraid to break up her family, however heavy the lie.

She wasn't naïve any more.

Everything she loved about her father had been a façade.

He'd lied. *To everyone*.

He'd cared for none of them. Only himself.

Just like Konstantinos.

She stepped back.

'I hate you,' she said, her voice devoid of anything.

The pulse throbbed in his clean-shaven cheek.

With her head held high, Poppy walked past him, and ignored the drag of his scent on her senses as she missed grazing his shoulder by millimetres.

She zeroed in on the limousine—ignored his looming presence at her heels.

The driver opened the door, and she climbed inside.

Her gaze locked to the figure closing in.

She yanked the door closed before he could get in beside her.

With a heavy exhale, she settled herself into the luxurious interior, let the plush cream leather support her newly found backbone.

She'd demand a divorce.

Konstantinos's skin prickled.

He didn't need to turn around to know her gaze was locked

on him. It bored into his back. So aware was he of his wife, of her smell, her presence, his body hummed from the balls of his feet to his scalp.

He swallowed thickly and pulled free a crystal stopper from the decanter, and spilt two fingers' worth of a deep amber-coloured spirit into two glasses. He collected them, and only then did he turn.

Her back straight, her knees together, she sat in a high-back, winged chair. Her slender arms resting on the white velvet, she met his gaze dead on. She didn't look towards the floor-to-ceiling window, or the view of the Eiffel Tower right outside.

He'd tracked her here. *Her rings*. He'd lost her again, the trail cold, but he'd known she was still here. In France. He could feel it. He'd bought *this* penthouse, because so sure had he been he'd find her. In this place they'd met. *Paris*.

Never would he have considered she was with Léon.

He gritted his teeth. He should have stayed away all those years ago. Away from the Durands. Away from *her*. Because when the opportunity had arisen to claim her, he had. He'd offered her a job close to him. Everywhere he'd gone, so had she.

He'd thought *that* would be enough.

He'd convinced himself the more he saw of her, the more she'd become commonplace. *Invisible*. It would ease, he'd told himself. The need to have her. But it didn't. In London, her mouth had been too near. The pink pout, burnt onto his retinas, had been too tempting.

He'd leaned in too far—

Fire shot through his veins.

He'd noticed her long before she'd come to be in the meeting at Durand Towers. He'd feared *she* was the reason he kept going back, doing deals he never usually would for a glimpse of her. But he'd dismissed it. He did not want blindly. His lovers were usually widows—women who didn't want what he wouldn't give. *Marriage*.

Their affair had been like nothing he'd ever experienced. He'd met no one like her. So strong in her convictions had she been. *Her rules.* Their relationship would not interfere with her job. She wanted him. *Only sex.* She didn't want love or emotion. She didn't want marriage, or children.

She had been his mirror image.

Rules. They were so important to them both.

Her dad had been an adulterous bastard. He'd made Poppy feel unsafe in her own home. In a home that should have been her haven, he'd made her walk on a knife's edge, waiting for the next affair. Always making her feel at risk he'd leave. *That* was the power of love. It was selfish. It made others hurt.

It killed them.

His love had killed his mother.

He'd promised he would never hurt *Poppy.*

He would never have the power to, because he'd never love her, as she had promised never to love him.

They'd both wanted the same thing…a life led honourably alone.

He had told her things—confessed things he'd told no one. His hatred for his father. It was their commonality.

She'd become his confidante. *His friend.*

She'd been hiding in plain sight. Out there. *So close.*

He walked towards her.

She didn't blink, and neither did he.

She wouldn't bolt again.

Not until he knew she was safe.

He wouldn't have another death on his conscience. His mother's death pressed on his shoulders every day. A weight he carried through each stroke of his morning swim.

In another life, he would have saved his mother.

In this life, he would have to save everyone else.

He'd tried to save Poppy.

He knew she battled with her own current. He knew the tide

had been too strong for her when Isaak had died. It had taken her under with him. Into darkness. Her mental health after the funeral was so very...*poor*.

Was it still?

He stood before her.

Flowers.

The scent flooded his senses. Burnt its way into his nostrils.

Theos mou...

He handed down the glass to her sitting form. 'Drink this.'

Her slender fingers rose, long and elegant, and she tentatively took it from his grasp, cupping it from the bottom and purposefully missing his fingers.

He released it to her.

Together, they brought the thick crystal to their mouths. In sync, their lips opened as the crystal tilted. The amber fire spilt onto his tongue. Her throat flexed.

His drained, the glass fell from his mouth, and he placed it down on the long-legged occasional table beside her.

She finished the rest of her drink, and put it beside his. And oh, so slowly, she put her hands, palm side down, on the armrests of the chair. She pushed her knees from their bent position.

So small, she stood before him.

She looked like his wife. She smelt like her. But...she was different. *Changed*.

An unknown—*unfamiliar*—energy vibrated from her too slight frame.

And it was...*too big*.

She didn't look like the Poppy on the cliff.

Her eyes glittered.

The silent drag of breath through her slightly flared nostrils made her chest rise too slowly. And it pulsed in the silence between them.

Anger. But *his* Poppy didn't silently seethe. His Poppy didn't recoil from his touch. *His* Poppy would have opened her mouth and caressed his fingers with her tongue. *Sucked them.*

His wife would have let him have her in the alleyway.

His wife did not hate *him*. The man he was with her. The man he'd spent years honing. An honest man. A man who promised to protect. A man who'd tried to protect her.

You failed her.

You failed him.

He wouldn't think of the tiny casket.

He wouldn't think of the weightless box on his shoulder as he carried it to a grave too small.

He would not again admit the truth that he had manifested his infant son's death. He'd caused it, because never should he have allowed it. For him to be conceived when he knew his genes were defective.

His jaw firmed.

He was dead.

His death did not matter.

He had never been part of the plan, anyway.

His stomach revolted at his declaration of indifference.

She raised her neck too sharply, and said, without inflection, 'I want a divorce.'

He caught it. The fall of his jaw.

'You do not want a divorce,' he dismissed, keeping the edge from his tone.

'I do.' Shoulders back, she stepped forward.

He stepped back. *Fractionally.* He wouldn't give her the space—*the room*—to claim an opportunity to run again, but he'd give her the illusion she wasn't trapped.

'Why would you want to keep me?' Naturally, arched eyebrows rose. 'I hate you,' she repeated, the French roll of her vowels enunciating each sharp point of her words.

'You already said,' he replied flatly, but he flinched inwardly.

How many times had his mother called his father a liar? *A*

bastard? Told him she hated him? His father had deserved her hate. Her venom. He'd broken her. Driven her into the sea. But *he* didn't deserve…*this*.

He'd never hurt Poppy.

Didn't you?

His breathing faltered.

No. He'd stuck to the rules. He'd done everything he'd promised.

Poppy wasn't herself.

She hadn't been for too long.

He dipped his gaze to the pulse thrumming beneath her skin. He wanted to touch it—feather his fingers down her throat and close his palm over the pulse he knew beat for him.

'It isn't hate you feel.' His gaze flitted back to hers. 'It's *want.*'

'You're wrong,' she spat.

'No,' he said. 'I'm not.'

'You disgust me.'

'I do not disgust you,' he said, too tightly. *Too breathlessly.*

She leaned in. 'You do.' She feathered her fingers across his right pectoral.

Hunger he'd repressed too deeply flooded through him. Acute and intense, it pulled tight every muscle in his body.

'But if you need me to…' Her breasts brushed against him. The tightened tips beneath her shirt, making his jaw tighten to stem the itch to do what he wanted. Pop each button of her cotton shirt, pull down her bra, and expose them to his mouth. *His tongue.* Her flushed pink aureoles. Her taut nipples.

A hunger he'd only ever known with her speared through him.

He closed his eyes.

It had been too long…

His body pulsed. The memory of the last time he'd been with her shredded the curtain of time. His mind remembered and his body felt it. The thought of burying himself inside her after months of abstaining tightened his groin.

Months, and he hadn't touched her.

She had not touched him.

He'd understood the dangers of sex while she was on bedrest. He knew her body needed to be protected so she could nourish their son. But after the funeral, still she had not come to him. Her depression so heavy, he'd left her to the professionals. The nurses. The doctor. The therapist.

Guilt prodded his temples.

Had he helped her enough?

Yes. He alone hadn't been enough to save her. He could not break the cycle of depression. He didn't know how to. He hadn't known how to end her grief. And so he'd stayed away.

But *that* day, so famished for the silken fist of her body, he'd driven himself inside her in agonised thrusts of desperation.

He hadn't even taken her panties off. He'd pulled them aside, lifted her against the wall, and she'd wrapped her legs around him. Welcomed his heat with a scream he had caught in his mouth. Swallowed into his lungs.

He'd lost control.

They'd both come so hard. *So fast.*

The first time they'd had sex in months.

The last time he'd had sex for over a year now.

She hadn't come to him again. Not long after that day, she'd left him.

He opened his eyes. Met the wide blue of hers.

'If I need what?' he pressed stiffly.

She tilted her neck to look up at him. Her lips were so close. The cool, sweet air leaving her mouth feathered his own, and his lips parted of their own volition. He needed only to dip his head and taste her.

'Proof,' she said, and rose on the balls of her feet, 'why I'd never *want* you again.' The palm of her right hand on his shoulder, her other hand swept further along his chest and disappeared inside his jacket.

His mind scrambled. Her touch, her parted lips… They contradicted her every word.

He swallowed. So quickly did she turn him on. So quickly did she undo him.

He hardened. *Everywhere.*

His brain turned to fuzz as everything pulsed. 'What are you talking about?' he husked, his body an assault of senses.

'*This.*' She stepped back, and clenched tightly in her hand was his phone.

Her head ducked. Her hair fell forward as she illuminated the screen with the flick of her thumb.

'You little pickpocket,' he breathed.

'Tell me the pin.'

'Why would you steal my phone?'

'You wouldn't have given it to me if I'd asked.'

'But why do you want it?'

'I don't have mine,' she answered flippantly.

'I'll retrieve yours for you.'

'*Pin?*' she repeated.

His gaze narrowed. He took in the heightened flush to her cheeks. The tremble in her fingers holding his phone.

'Fine.' He rattled off a number.

He watched her open apps, enter codes for a long minute, before her fingers stilled.

She held out his phone. 'Look familiar?'

His gaze flicked to the screen. It was *him.* 'Of course.'

He remembered *that* afternoon. How could he forget? His father had died.

In the photo, his shoulders were too tight as he sat outside, because the smell indoors, he could no longer demand his lungs to inhale it. The smell he could never quite wash off. Cloying, it lingered in his hair—*his clothes*—inside the walls of his nostrils. *Death.*

'And what about this one?' Her thumb swiped against the screen. Another photo appeared of the same place, same time, with Isabella's lips pressed against his.

He dragged his gaze to hers.

The accusation in her eyes…

He snatched air into his lungs.

Clarity. It bled into his consciousness. It flooded through him with razor-sharpness.

She wasn't sad.

She wasn't sick.

He'd believed she'd left him because of Isaak. He'd believed every time she looked at him, she saw what she'd lost. What he could not save. Their son.

The air left his lungs in a rush.

'You think I was having sex with *her*?'

'I don't think anything,' she said, her gaze locked on the screen between them. '*I know.*'

CHAPTER THREE

KONSTANTINOS KNEW SHE'D grown up in a house of lies. It was part of her rules. Their agreement. No one else. Only them. *Loyalty.*

It had been so for the entirety of their marriage.

Before and after, she'd run away.

Five long years of just *her.*

'You know what, exactly, *glikia mou*?' he asked. 'You haven't asked me anything.'

He'd protected her, kept the truth from her, because it was a truth she couldn't handle. The death of his father. He hadn't wanted to expose her to any more death. It had surrounded her for weeks. They'd only buried Isaak days before he'd found out his father was dying. And he'd done everything in his power to keep more death from her life.

Liar. You closed the door as she wept.

His gut gripped in a tight fist.

He couldn't grieve with her.

He'd had to keep functioning.

You didn't even comfort her.

He couldn't. He couldn't listen to her cry and not…*feel.* And the threat of *that.* He could not risk it. Feelings fixed nothing.

He'd hired nurses while she was pregnant on bedrest so she could stay at home and not remain in the private hospital on the mainland. He'd avoided her, because he was afraid those feelings of hers—the worry—*the nesting*—the feelings she so obviously felt for the child in her womb would somehow make their way inside him. *Infect him.* Make him react. Make him…*feel.*

He couldn't allow *that.*

He'd needed to keep his head the way he hadn't been able to do with his mother. His feelings had made him panic. He'd let his mother down because he'd let feelings seep in. Take over when he should have remained in control.

He'd vowed he would stay in control thereafter. He'd sworn to protect Poppy and their son. But she'd lost—

His breath caught. She hadn't lost Isaak. He had died. And a part of her… Something had died in her too. He'd hired doctors, mental-health professionals to bring back the Poppy she had been.

You turned your back on her.

His chest heaved.

He'd felt as helpless in the face of her grief and depression as he had with her mother's. *He'd known.* But he'd done everything he could. Given her everything she'd needed. Professional help. His mother hadn't had it. Had never been offered it. She had died.

He'd kept Poppy alive.

And her distrust…

It was betrayal, and it cut him bone-deep.

'You abandoned our marriage because of a photograph? You condemned me without a hearing.'

'Photos don't lie.'

'Neither do I.'

'That's *you*,' she said. 'That's *your* mouth on hers.' She jabbed her finger at the screen, bringing the image back to its full, sharpest, brightest intensity. 'She was my replacement in every way, wasn't she? Your PA when I became your wife…' She swallowed, as if the words crawling up her throat physically harmed her. 'She'd taken over my job. She was there every day in your office, tempting you with everything I was withholding.' Betrayal laced every word. '*Sex*.'

'We had sex,' he reminded her.

'*Once*,' she countered thickly. 'In months.'

He gritted his teeth. Neither of them had wanted a conventional marriage, because of their pasts. They had both wanted one person they could rely on who knew the rules. No emotional complications, but security, loyalty. And they'd both known what would hold their marriage together. *Sex*. And it had been so.

Until the accident.

The birth control had failed. *He'd* failed. But their baby had been made. And so it was done. Her pregnancy at high risk of placental abruption. Sex was off the table, but he'd *never* strayed.

He'd watched her body grow.

He'd got his head around the fact he was going to be a father. He would have an heir. The Ariti line would continue without the influence of his father's cruelty or his mother's illness. *He* was going to do it differently. And then…

His heart squeezed.

Isaak was no more.

He hadn't needed sex with another woman. He had needed his wife. He'd needed normality. Life to continue as it had been before, but Poppy had just…*stopped*. Stopped living.

'You wanted proof.' She shook the phone, raised it a little higher. 'And here it is. You lie to everyone,' she accused. 'You pretend to be honest—*honourable*. And it's all a pretence. *A lie*.'

Her words ground into his temples.

His whole life he'd made himself be honourable. Never deceitful, like his father. He kept his word. *Always*. And she'd abandoned him anyway. Just like his mother. She'd left him behind… A man trained to be…*perfect*.

He inched closer to her. Took the phone from her clenched

fingertips. He turned the screen to her. 'Do you know where this photograph was taken?'

'Why would it matter where you took another woman to bed?'

Why did it matter that she knew? That he told her? He knew the answers, didn't he?

Tonight, he'd tried to remove the last shred of softness inside him.

He *had* to become his father to prevent himself from feeling… *pain*. But the man he'd tried to kill tonight in Léon's dining room, his soul still lingered inside him, seeking validation for the life he'd tried to end. That he was still needed. *Was he?*

His jaw firmed. The man he'd nurtured into adulthood after his mother's death hung on by his fingernails, clawing at his flesh from the inside out, demanding he be calm—that he explain. And so he did. *Roughly.*

'Hospital grounds are not my preference for foreplay.'

'Why were you at a hospital with *her*?'

'I was working.' He shrugged. 'The world did not stop turning because I was waiting for him to die.'

Her whole face frowned. 'Who was dying?'

'*This* photograph was taken moments after my father was pronounced dead.'

She visibly shook herself. 'Your dad's dead?'

'Yes, as you would have known if you'd waited to ask me why I was sitting on the terrace of a private hospital. But you didn't ask, did you, Poppy? You didn't wait for me to tell you she kissed me and I pushed her away.'

He turned off the screen and put it back into his pocket.

'You were simply gone.'

Poppy reeled.

He'd never lied to her before. Even in the beginning, he'd told her the truth. It was the core of their connection. He was painfully honest. He hadn't sugar-coated his surprise at the pregnancy. He'd told her the truth. He'd never wanted a baby. *Still didn't.* But it was done. And he'd do his duty to her and the child.

Provide and protect.

He'd never made false promises.

It pummelled something in her chest. Her actions. She'd been so sure…

After the funeral, she'd been such a mess. Time had no meaning. Most of the time she hadn't known what day it was. What season. But she'd known, with the clearest clarity, Konstantinos wasn't there.

She was sick, and he was gone.

His absence grew more acute in her consciousness when the medication had eased the fog surrounding her every thought. It had become her obsession to find out exactly what he was doing when he didn't come home. And why, when he did, he'd headed straight for the shower…

She'd needed help to do it.

She'd hired the private investigator.

A week later, the photos had been all she'd needed.

She hadn't known it was a private hospital.

She'd never followed up with the PI.

It would have been easy to do, but she'd called Serena.

She'd abandoned her phone—*abandoned her life*—because the photos had told her a story. Confirmed her every suspicion he was doing exactly what her father had done to her mum.

But Konstantinos hadn't been unfaithful.

He'd had the opportunity and pushed the other woman away.

It was whiplash.

Poppy believed him.

But if he'd told her the truth…

'Your dad,' she said huskily. 'Don't you think I had a right to know?'

'He wasn't your father.'

'No, he was yours,' she countered, her heart thumping. 'And I was your wife.'

'You *are* my wife.'

His declaration shook her on her feet. He'd dislodged her every assumption. But her instincts hadn't lied to her, had they?

He had.

He'd been hiding something from her. *Something big.* And if he could lie by omission? If he could hide the fact he was waiting for his father to die from his wife—*from her*—what else was he hiding? What other secrets had he kept from her?

She didn't want to be the last to know or, worse, die in ignorance, like her mum.

Lying, it was a trigger for her. So many lies had raised her into the woman she was. *Guarded.* But he'd got beneath her defences. He'd made her believe she could have him if nothing else. *Only him.* Not a family. Not children.

Never had she wanted to risk a child feeling the way she had growing up. As if her position in a family—*her family*—was conditional.

She knew now, because of Isaak, she'd never let *that* happen to a child of hers, but...

Her stomach ached.

It would never not ache.

There would never be another baby. But there would always be some type of pain. That was how the world worked. It dished out hope and took it away in the blink of an eye. And when she was hurting again—when the world decided to take another swipe, brought her down to her knees again...

Where would *he* be?

She'd barely seen him after they'd lost their baby. She'd thought he was avoiding her. She'd thought he was having an affair. But he'd chosen to be beside a man he hated while she was...*hurting.*

Yes, he'd hired professionals. But he'd promised she could

rely on him. *Trust him.* But she couldn't. Not when it really mattered. Not when she needed him.

'I still want a divorce,' she said.

His jaw sharpened to cut steel. 'You *still* want a divorce?'

'Yes.' Her heart thrummed to a beat that pulsed too loud. *Too fast.* It was frantic. And it hurt. Behind her breastbone. He'd abandoned her to strangers to ease his conscience. He hadn't cared about his father. He hadn't cared about his son. He had not cared about *her.*

He cared for no one but himself.

For that, she couldn't forgive him.

'I do,' she breathed.

'No.'

'No?'

'There will be no divorce.' His lips lifted to bare his teeth. 'I am Konstantinos Ariti, your husband, and you will return to *me. You* will repair the damage you have done to my reputation. You will show them you are safe. You will show them I did not abandon my duty. You will show them I am the man who protects his own when they are weak—when they are sick. You will show them all you are alive.'

Confusion contorted her face. It was his ethos—to protect his people. It was what he wanted the world to see, even if it was a lie, but—

'Show who?'

'The press,' he enlightened her.

She blinked rapidly. 'The press?'

She hadn't read a newspaper—looked online—in so long. Not since the photo of her standing on the cliff's edge looking into the sea after the funeral.

She wasn't going to jump.

She'd just wanted…

She didn't know.

Standing up there, she'd understood why the monks had

chosen the so very difficult to reach island of Sotiría to search for their sacred solitude. She'd understood why Konstantinos had renovated the abandoned white brick monastery to become their home.

It stood centrally within the green land mass, but hermitages—simple three-walled structures—were scattered throughout the island for when the monks had sat with nothing but themselves and the island for contemplation. And she'd stood there outside of the three-columned walls of the one at the top, overlooking all of Sotiría.

The stillness…never had she known anything so absent of chatter. But the island sang with a different noise. The pine-covered cliffs, the white sands contrasting with the crystal-blue sea, they'd all hummed. But she'd felt nothing. Not the wind throwing her hair into her face or plastering the thin cotton of her dress to her body. She hadn't recognised the danger of the incoming storm or how close her bare feet had come to the edge.

She had just felt…*empty*.

But their headlines had been cutting alongside the stolen image of her standing there…

'*You* will show them you are, and always have been, safe, and are my devoted wife,' he said, jolting her back from the cliff's edge.

'You want me to lie to them?'

'Yes,' he husked, his chest rising and deflating in short, powerful pumps of his lungs.

'You want me to make them think we're still together? Pretend nothing's happened?' She swallowed. 'For *your* reputation?'

'Yes.' He stepped closer. 'I had planned to spend some time in Paris,' he continued, 'to rejoin society after the takeover of Léon's organisation, to change the narrative expressed daily online, in the papers, but now *you* will change it for me. We will implement a PR campaign of you attending chosen events. *This* will correct the headlines that you are hidden somewhere on the island because I have let you fall into despair. You will show them that all you needed was time, but you are back, *stronger*, by my side,' he snarled. 'And you will start tomorrow, when we attend the première of *Incapable de Voler*.'

'You want me to attend…' she frowned in disbelief '…*a play*?'

'Ballet opera at the Palais Garnier,' he corrected. 'A small select group will be in attendance. Important dignitaries. Celebrities. And…*us*.'

'I can't.' Panic flared in her chest. 'The press will be there in droves.'

'That is why *we* will be there.'

She could imagine the cold and callous headlines about *them*. The articles ripping their marriage apart with horrible assumptions about her disappearance from public life. But she didn't want to be part of their daily harassment schedule again. *Ever*.

'I can't do it.'

'And why not, *poulaki mou*?'

'Because too much has happened to paint on a smile and—' she heaved in a heavy breath '—pretend everything is okay. *It isn't!*'

'You married me to help my image,' he reminded her. '*You* will remain married to me to fix it.'

Something died inside her.

He'd searched the world to find her, but he didn't want *her* to come back to him.

Had some part of her hoped he wanted her back?

No. But still, it stung. After everything they'd been through, he wanted her to play a part. Put on a show. For *his* reputation. He wanted her to lie to the world to restore his image. The thought of doing it—putting on a show of smiles and tiaras—and pretending her son, however briefly he'd been with her, hadn't changed her. Changed everything.

He had.

She wouldn't betray her son.

She would not forget him.

Not like…*him.*

'I won't lie.' She shook her head. 'Not even for *you.*'

You've lied before.

Shame heated her cheeks. She'd done it for her father. *For herself*, she corrected. But she didn't want to be that person any more. She wouldn't be her.

A liar.

Konstantinos knew the vague truth about her family—her father's adulterous ways—but he didn't know *her* part in destroying two families. And she wouldn't tell him.

She couldn't.

'Is it a lie to show them how we once were?' he asked softly. A voice intended to soothe. *To seduce.* 'To show them how we couldn't keep our hands off each other? How strong our connection—'

'Stop it,' she husked, because she didn't want to think of the before.

It was done.

It was over.

They were over.

'Is it so terrible to re-enact something that was once true?' he asked. 'We can jump back—rewind time to before—'

'*Isaak?*' His name flew from her mouth. She waited for him to say it back. His name. He never had after he'd gone.

Isaak's name meant *laughter.*

Konstantinos had chosen it. A name he now refused to speak. But she'd known when he'd walked into her room and announced it. She'd known why he'd chosen it. Their childhoods had been void of laughter. *Of light.* They both knew those truths about each other. Both knew their childhoods were why they'd needed a marriage set within boundaries.

They had been so similar in so many ways, and yet…

She was different now. Before Isaak, never would she have cried. Let herself…*feel*. But she felt. Felt too much. And she couldn't stop them. *Feelings*. She didn't want to stop. Her grief was her connection to Isaak. Her son. To the love she never knew she could feel this intensely—this achingly—for anyone. But she had loved her son. *Loved him*.

'*We* will spend the week here,' he responded, as if she'd never said his name out loud. As if he meant nothing.

He'd never wanted a baby, she reminded herself.

But you did.

She hadn't. Not until she'd felt him growing inside her. And she'd sworn he would know everything she hadn't. *Stability*. No one would threaten to yank her love away from her child. Her child would not have to keep secrets to earn her love. She'd love him. *Unconditionally*. And then her stomach had been as empty as her heart. And Konstantinos had just carried on. As if the death of their child meant nothing.

She closed her eyes briefly. *Shut him out.*

She wouldn't think of it.

She wouldn't let it hurt her while he watched and pretended their son had never existed.

They could never go back to their original agreement.

There was too much ugliness between them now. Too much unsaid. *Too much pain*. She didn't have the words, she knew. Didn't know how to explain how his indifference to what they'd lost…

It was a hurt he could never fix.

'You will lie, Poppy, and you'll make them believe it,' he said. 'Then we will go home.'

She opened her eyes. '*Home?*'

'We'll return to Greece.'

'I'm not going back to Greece.'

'But you are,' he contradicted her. 'And there, back in our

marital home, you will prepare for an event. An event so spectacular—*so very beautiful*—for the renewal of our vows.'

'The renewal of our vows?' she repeated. Dumbfounded.

He turned his back on her. 'We'll leave no one in doubt about the strength of our marriage.'

'Our marriage is over,' she said to his back.

'Choose any of the bedrooms,' he said over his shoulder. 'Tomorrow you will repair the damage you have caused by running away from me without cause, and blaming me for something *I* did not do.'

'We're not finished talking about this.'

'I am.'

He walked out of the door.

'Konstantinos!'

CHAPTER FOUR

Poppy's nose pinched.

She wouldn't cry. But it threaded through her, the need to release the tension pulling her face muscles tight.

What had she expected? That he'd let her go without damage control? Damage control was his personality. To take control. To fix everything. *For everyone.*

She let out a self-mocking laugh.

She'd liked that about him in the beginning—was attracted to his unwavering need to make decisions that were fair for everyone, but *this* wasn't fair.

When had his every decision become so self-serving? *Selfish?*

When had Konstantinos become a...*stranger*?

She didn't recognise him any more. Not the man who had been in Léon's dining room and not the man demanding she go to bed and wake up as his wife.

She tugged her bottom lip between her teeth.

He'd become someone different the minute she'd told him she was pregnant. Distanced himself. Ended every conversation when she'd still been speaking. Taken control when all she'd needed was for him to listen.

And she'd let him.

She'd let him put her in a room at the furthest point of the monastery when the doctor had told him she needed complete bedrest. She'd let him hire nurses to stand guard at *her* bed. Not their bed any more. Not *their* room.

He'd played God from a different room—ordered her life into something manageable where he didn't have to take an active part. He'd managed *her*. He'd pushed her away—forgotten about her—until she simply wasn't there.

Until she'd run.

Her eyes travelled to the gold doors of the private lift.

She could run again.

She snatched a too shallow breath through her nostrils.

He'd find her.

He needed her back.

He needed her to lie for him.

But what did *she* need?

Not this. She didn't want to be in the public eye again. She didn't want to be his wife again, but maybe she was being selfish, too. Didn't she owe him a little damage control? Didn't she owe it to herself? To close the door on the last five years of her life and know she never had to open it again? Never had to look over her shoulder to see if her past was catching up with her?

She'd run away and buried her head. Pretended it would all go away. As she always had.

Konstantinos wasn't going away.

Unless she…

She could let herself pretend, couldn't she? *Just this once.* He was the Konstantinos she'd met so many years ago. She could appeal to *him*. Offer *him* a fair contract as he had offered to her. She'd offer him a deal where everyone got what they wanted. Where everyone got to walk away with their pride intact.

And Léon?

Her heart clenched.

He was her *only* friend now.

She owed him.

She would get him out of it, too.

She'd get them *both* out.

Heart hammering, Poppy went to find her husband.

The corridor was a maze of doors, but only one stood ajar.

She moved towards it.

She stopped before it, raised her hand, formed it into a fist and…

The door moved.

Inch by inch, it opened.

'I'll do it,' she said, before he came into view, and she changed her mind.

He stood in the doorway. His jacket had been removed, another button on his shirt undone, revealing a dusting of fine dark hairs.

She swallowed tightly—ignored the embers of heat low in her stomach.

'Do what, *glikia mou*?' he asked, as if it was already decided.

'I'll play whatever game you want to play to mess with the press,' she said, because they deserved to be duped. 'I'll help you change whatever narrative the paparazzi have imposed on your life about our separation.'

'And what do you want in return?'

'Your signature on our divorce papers,' she demanded, 'and I want Léon's debt signed over to me.'

'To do what with it?'

'To rip it up,' she said honestly.

His gaze narrowed. 'Why did you go to him?'

She squared her shoulders. Looked him dead in the eyes and told him the truth. 'He understood the grief of losing a son.'

And she waited for it. For words he'd never given her. Words she'd needed. An acknowledgement he'd lost Isaak, too.

The thump in his throat quickened. His angled chin jutted forward, only a fraction.

He said nothing.

Her heart hiccuped.

She couldn't force him to say words he didn't mean. Words her heart longed for.

'It's a good offer,' she said. She hated the tightness in her throat. 'It's a fair offer. *Reasonable*. Everyone gets what they want—what they need,' she said thickly. 'I'll be your adoring wife in public in exchange—'

'And in private?' he interjected, his voice a low husk of temptation that arrowed straight to her pelvis.

He stepped aside.

Her eyes flicked to the four-poster bed behind him.

It was magnificent. Bare oak, carved in intricate spirals.

Her insides twisted into knots of hate and desire.

Oh, how easy it would be to offer her traitorous body to his treacherous plum lips.

She shook her hair behind her back and straightened her spine. 'Nothing happens,' she proclaimed.

Thick brows rose. 'Are you sure?' he asked, but his eyes, they spoke to her flesh. To her lips. To the body that yearned to be his one last time.

Her eyes locked on to the bed. The big white pillows, the crisp cotton…

Loneliness. It was the worst hurt. It was visceral. A war inside her that demanded she surrender to it. Crawl into bed with him. And let him—*what*?

He'd never offered his arms when she'd needed them most.

She wouldn't need him now.

Her throat dried. 'I'm sure,' she said, but words were easy to say, and easier to forget. 'If we do this, I want it in writing, Konstantinos. I want a contract.'

'A contract?'

'Legal documentation.'

The pulse in his jaw throbbed. 'My word isn't enough?'

'Not any more.'

The first time they'd got married in a spectacular event in

an Athens cathedral, she'd needed only his word. She'd thought their agreement would last forever, with no need for a way out. A way to end them.

She needed it now.

'I don't trust you,' she admitted. 'I want it in black and white. A contract outlining Léon's debt, and that you'll sign it over to me. I want to know the duration of the agreement and a list of what events I must attend, details of our sleeping arrangements—'

'And the sex?'

'The sex?'

'Am I to add a no-sex clause for the remaining duration of our marriage?'

Poppy held her breath and counted to ten.

If she didn't build a divide now, would she want to later?

She couldn't take *that* risk.

She didn't trust him not to change the rules if they weren't written down. But most of all she didn't trust herself.

'Yes.' She released a steady stream of air through her lips. 'Add it.'

It had been a tease. A flippant counter-argument to ask her if she wanted a no-sex clause in her preposterous request for a contract.

Konstantinos hadn't expected her to agree to it—*to demand it.*

He'd told her the truth. She'd dismissed it. As if it didn't matter. As if the reason she'd walked away—left him behind—was still reason enough to request a divorce. She didn't want him to touch her.

His chest heaved.

She didn't trust him.

Not to keep the vows of the marriage.

Not with her body.

A rage so hot—*so ferocious*—erupted inside Konstantinos's chest. Whatever chains had held him back—held his tongue in check—snapped. He couldn't contain it—*couldn't hold back*—the fire rising in his throat.

'This is not a business negotiation,' he said, each word a rough growl spoken from his chest. 'I am your husband. You are my wife. And you treat me like a stranger. As if I would take advantage of the things you don't want to give.'

Heat bloomed on her cheeks.

'You request these things as if I do not know the beauty spot beneath your left breast,' he continued, because he couldn't stop. 'As if I haven't kissed it with my mouth—felt its texture with my tongue.'

He watched the emotions flit across her face. The rise of heat blooming on her chest deepen the pinks on her already warm cheeks. The flare of her nostrils…

She wanted him. *Still.*

Her hands, so small, rose to her midriff, and she entwined her elegant fingers. Pressing her fingertips into her knuckles.

'You *are* a stranger to me, Konstantinos.'

It speared him in the chest.

Her dagger of indifference.

'I'm no stranger to you,' he hissed. 'I know every inch of your body. I know your scent. I know…*you.*'

'I don't recognise *you*,' she corrected.

'I have not changed,' he growled. 'I'm the man you—'

'You're cold, Konstantinos. *Selfish.* You don't care how hard it will be for me to go out there   ' she waved towards the lift at the end of the corridor '—in front of them.'

'You did not consider me, *agape*,' he said darkly, 'when you left me to answer questions I did not know the answer to.'

'You lied to *me*.' She placed her palm to the centre of her chest. As if he'd hurt her there.

Something inside him shifted. *Dropped.*

'I did not lie,' he said. *Roughly.*

'You didn't tell me about your dad.' She closed her eyes. Her chest rose sharply. Up and down. 'It doesn't matter.' She sighed. Opened her eyes. 'We're not the people we thought we were any more. And what you did to Léon tonight…' Her shoulders rose. *Squared.* '*That* is proof you're not the man I married. You're taking over Léon's company with no consideration of what *that* will do to him. You would have considered it… *before.* But now…you care for nothing but yourself.'

He closed his eyes—let the pump of his heart drown out everything.

He hadn't changed. He'd been everything he'd promised he would be. He'd protected her. *She* had changed. Every day with the swell of her stomach. She'd pushed him away.

Rage…it heated his skin.

Never did he lose his temper.

Never did he lose control.

It was a point of pride. To be in control of his emotions. His actions. His parents had been so reckless with theirs. His mother's despair. His father's relentless search for the ultimate power. It had corrupted them both. These…*emotions.* They had overwhelmed every aspect of their lives until they couldn't see anything else.

They couldn't see you.

Yes. It had been a hard truth in his childhood. It had been a hard truth when he had tried frantically to stay above the water with his mother's weight in his arms as the sea took him under. Again. And again.

He had felt it *that* day. Emotion. So thick. So overwhelming.

Emotion had caused his mother to drown.

He'd let her drown because he'd panicked.

He'd lost control.

He'd sworn never again to panic. Never again would he not see what was right in front of him. Never again would he be too late to protect those he loved because emotion had frozen him to the spot.

And so he'd chosen never to feel.

Never to love.

But it had seeped from his pores the moment he'd come home to find Poppy gone. He'd searched the world to find her, to put everything back where it was. Restore the life he'd built. And now she was here, and still he did not have it.

Control.

Blood roared in his ears.

He would have it.

He would take back his control.

But she was right.

He wasn't the man she'd married.

'Konstantinos?' Her voice was tentative—*quiet*—but it boomed in his ears, and his eyes, they opened.

His gaze drifted across the vulnerable softness of her mouth. He lifted his gaze, met the deep blue of hers. And her eyes, they were questioning. *Wary.*

Her distrust mocked his whole life.

It was a betrayal of his entire existence.

It erased the man he'd made himself become. An honest man. A man she could rely on. *Trust.* But she was abandoning him anyway. She wanted to leave him behind as if he was nothing. Like everyone else. His father. His mother…

It was because she saw it, didn't she?

She hadn't been running from the darkness in herself for all these months.

She'd been running from the darkness in *him.*

She saw what he'd tried to hide his whole life. The man beneath the suit. A man capable of unthinkable things. Not the man who tried to fix the world. Not the man who had wanted to fix *her.* But a man ready to let it fall to ruin, so he could stand on the apocalypse beneath him as king.

He'd never wanted to fix her, had he? She had been nothing but a cover-up. A façade to keep the lie of himself alive. He'd wanted to find her so he could continue to live the lie that he wasn't his father's son. But he *was*. And *he* couldn't be trusted.

He swallowed down the burn of rage in his throat.

'Then it is agreed,' he said, his voice a brutal husk.

'What is?'

'I'll give you all you have requested.'

She frowned. 'You will?'

He nodded. A too tight dip of his head. 'The agreement will last for one year.'

Her brows rose. '*A year?*'

'Three months of public appearances until the renewal of our vows,' he declared with an ease he didn't feel.

'And then?'

'*You* will stay on the island for the rest of our contract. *Alone*.'

Shadows grew inside the blue swirls of her irises. 'Alone?'

'I will commit to working engagements abroad.'

'You'll be working in another country?' Her nostrils flared. 'And I'll be…*there*?'

For the last year, they'd been apart. Not by his choice. This was his choice now. He was in control. He would use this year to restore everything she'd broken. And yet the idea of her in their home without him… It tugged at something in his chest. Made it ache.

He dismissed it.

'I will, of course, return in those nine months for the odd engagement where we will be seen together. We will have to continue to be seen in public as man and wife, but sporadically to make enough of a convincing PR campaign,' he said, changing tack, and *that* something in him eased. *A little*. 'At the end of the year, my reputation restored, we'll divorce. *Quietly*. We'll tell them the truth, that our marriage could not recover after the death of our son,' he continued, the admission in his mouth a heavy thing. Isaak had shattered everything. 'Then I'll set you free, *poulaki mou.*'

The silence pulsed.

'A year it is, Konstantinos,' she agreed.

He swallowed. *Heavily.* 'The contract will be ready tomorrow,' he said, and he knew in the morning he'd have figured it out. A way to take back the control she'd stolen from him.

So far, the plan was primitive.

He'd give her everything.

Then he'd take it all away.

'Goodnight, Poppy.'

Konstantinos closed the door in her face.

CHAPTER FIVE

The boned bodice of Poppy's dress felt like a too small cage.

Hunched over the laptop on her dressing table, she heaved, her chest pressing too tightly against the lace-ruffled trim.

She stared unblinkingly at the screen.

Konstantinos, he looked…

He didn't look like *him*.

She closed her eyes. Shut out the hundreds of images on her screen. Images of him. Endless open tabs of Konstantinos over the last year looking dishevelled. *Distracted*. In each photograph he looked…*tortured*.

She opened her eyes, looked down at the largest image in the centre of the screen. Konstantinos walking up the steps to his private jet. He'd turned. His black eyes shadowed. *Unseeing*.

The paparazzi had snapped him.

Never had she seen Konstantinos with a beard so unkempt.

Never had she seen him looking anything but pristine in public or private.

Image. It was everything to Konstantinos. So why was he not himself in any of these photographs? If his image was everything, why hadn't he cared what he looked like when he knew the paparazzi would create those awful articles? Articles she'd read all afternoon. They'd analysed his every frown. Every inch of his too long hair…

The knock at the door sent her pulse into overdrive.

Poppy's eyes snapped to the door.

It opened. He stood in the doorway in his perfect tux. She took in the sharp, angular jut of his jaw. His perfect face.

Still, she caught her breath.

Still, her stomach flipped.

He stepped into the room. 'It's time.'

'I need my shawl,' she said thickly.

His gaze flicked to the screen at her back.

She turned to it. Closed the lid. Collected her silver shawl and diamond clutch from where they sat next to the laptop. She turned back…

Her hand reached out automatically to steady herself. Solid heat met her palm. Her gaze flicked up to his.

His eyes dropped to her hand on his chest. 'I have something for you.'

'What?'

He didn't answer. He caught her wrist and brought it between their bodies. His touch was a light hold, barely there, but it snatched the air from her lungs.

He reached into his pocket. 'Did you really think I wouldn't recognise them?' To the tip of her ring finger he held her engagement ring. A green emerald and diamond trilogy set in silver platinum, and her wedding band.

'I found them in Maël Bijoux.'

She gasped. The famous French jeweller only specialised in unique antique jewellery. She had *not* sold them to *that* jeweller. She'd known it would be a risk to do so.

'*How?*' she breathed. 'How do you have them?'

He slipped them on. 'Jewellery of this calibre is sold to those who know its worth, not—' he released her hand and stepped back '—to common street traders who lend money to the poor at inflated prices for their television sets.'

She flushed. She'd chosen a common brand of French pawn brokers and taken a much lower price than their value, she knew, but…

'I needed the money,' she confessed huskily.

'You would have needed nothing if you'd taken your purse,' he answered coldly. 'My team tracked the rings when they came up for auction. I bought them back. But after the rings, the trail was dead.' He spread his hands wide. 'I bought this place and waited for the trail to be resurrected. Little did I know you were so close all along.'

She spread her fingers. Looked down at the rings. Her hand felt...*balanced.*

She looked at him. Took in his perfectly styled hair, combed back from his face. The clean-shaven jaw. He hadn't looked like this in the photos. A too long beard had hidden his face. He'd looked like someone else. And the press...the speculation... They'd questioned everything. His business decisions. *Their* marriage. *Her* role in his dishevelled appearance—his mental health.

They'd ripped into every aspect of his life. What had been *their* life... They'd used the photo of her again on the cliff, and concluded Konstantinos was either a madman who'd locked his wife up to keep her away from the public, or he'd lost her with his son and was keeping the news out of the press that she'd taken her own life. The death of his father, they'd called the *'final blow'*.

He'd built an empire on the foundations of protecting *his* people. *This* narrative would have destroyed him. To be accused of covering up her death. To be compared to his father. He hated his father. Everything he represented. *Brutality.*

She'd asked Léon not to tell or show her anything. No newspapers, no internet. She'd barricaded herself inside with nothing but her flowers and talk shows discussing other people's problems, and she'd ignored her own. Ignored how her disappearance had affected *him*. But seeing Konstantinos like *that...* almost...*sad...*

She'd never seen him sad. Never seen him cry, not with a sleeping Isaak in his arms, not at the funeral when she hadn't stopped crying. Not when she'd fallen to her knees from the weight of grief in her chest at the funeral.

But in *these* photos…he was visibly…*distraught*.

Emotion threatened to choke her.

She sidestepped him and hurried to the lift. She cradled her clutch to her chest as he took his place beside her. As the door opened and they stepped inside. Stood side by side, so close, but so far apart.

The lift doors opened. She stepped out into the marble foyer of twisted columns, and she kept walking under the stained-glass-roofed reception area. The click of her heels echoed behind her as they made their way to the waiting limousine. Doormen with dipped heads opened the doors. They climbed into their opposite sides.

The doors closed them in.

The car moved.

Paris, it blurred in front of her like a too fast fairground ride. Bright. *Vivid.*

Colour. She'd dotted her life with it. With flowers. With scents of hope after Isaak died. But she had been nothing but a shadow these last months. Living a monochromatic existence. And now he was taking her into the light. Taking her off life support and demanding she…*live.*

Konstantinos rattled something off in French to the driver.

The divider closed. And it was too small—the back of the car—it was too claustrophobic. Too full of *him*. Too full of the past.

She closed her eyes briefly.

The images and articles she'd scoured swirled in front of her eyes.

She resisted the urge to cover her mouth with her hand, and hold in her muffled cry of thick guilt in her throat.

'What is it?' he asked. 'What's wrong, Poppy?'

'I looked at the articles about you. About me. *About us.*'

'And?'

'They were…' She turned from the window.

He observed her with an intensity both sharp, and acute. 'They were what?'

'Disgusting.'

'They were,' he agreed. 'That's the point, Poppy. Tonight, we change the narrative and call them all liars.'

'Everything they said about us…*you*,' she said unevenly. 'I knew the articles wouldn't be good, but I hadn't expected them to be so…*vile*.'

'It's nothing you haven't seen them do before,' he dismissed. 'That's the nature of the press, unless you control them. We will squash the rumours I've hidden your suicide from the public. We will call every single one of their articles a lie. *That* is our PR strategy. Simple. Effective.'

She wanted to claw their eyes out. The soulless paparazzi who'd hounded him. She wanted to make sure they could never look through their camera lenses again and hurt him.

'I don't want you to talk about it any more,' he dismissed.

It was a gut punch.

He never had. Not when her body was broken. Not when her soul was shredded. Not when all she'd had was her words. Her heart squeezed. He'd paid someone else to listen for him. But…

'*You* asked me what was wrong,' she reminded him.

He moved in closer, until his thigh pressed against hers. It was firm. It was warm. It penetrated her. The solidity of him. 'And now you have told me the problem,' he said. 'I am done listening.'

She snatched a breath. There he was. The man she had run from. The man he *really* was. *Cold*. Before the baby he would have listened to her. Late at night, tangled in the sheets, he would have let her speak. About her mum. Her dad. *Her feelings*.

Images of every time she'd wanted to talk about the baby growing in her womb—the baby who was in danger inside her—flashed in her mind. The moment they'd been told the baby was at risk if she didn't have complete rest, he'd diagnosed her physical needs, provided the room, the bed, the nurse and closed his ears to her worry—looked away from her need to talk about it.

To talk about Isaak.

'You're a cold-hearted *bastard*!'

He shrugged. His hand rose. He claimed her chin between his thumb and forefinger. It was not a hold that hurt, but it was firm. He let the heat from his touch penetrate her skin. 'Do I feel cold to you, *poulaki mou*?'

Her every nerve—her every synapse—responded to it. *His closeness.*

He dipped his head.

It was instinct.

A demand of her body she couldn't deny.

She closed her eyes. 'Konstantinos…' she said, and she didn't know what it meant. His name on her lips. Was she warning him? Or herself?

He pressed his mouth to hers. And she knew she shouldn't move her lips. She should shut her mouth tightly. But she didn't. She leaned into the pressure of his mouth. His swiped against the entrance of hers.

And the hands which, somewhere in her consciousness, she knew she should raise to his chest and push him away, didn't. They left her lap and moulded to the solid wall of his chest. She smoothed her fingers over every rippled indentation.

His fingers released her chin. Feathered across her jaw. '*Glikia mou*,' he said into her mouth.

His lips moved. Pressed harder. Forced her mouth wider. With the open palm of his hand on the nape of her neck, he pulled her in closer. *Nearer.* And she felt…*enclosed.* In heat. In sensation.

She opened for him. Let the tip of his tongue thrust its way inside. It filled her mouth. She caught it with her own. Played with it. Danced with it.

It was a dance her body fell into step with without need of prompting. Without a reminder. She didn't have to learn his lips, because she knew every dip. And she traced them.

Their kiss hadn't been like this their last time together.

Months after the funeral, *that* kiss had been a battle of unspoken words.

This kiss…

It was old, but it was new.

It was a rewrite of *that* last time.

He thrust his tongue deeper into her mouth, as if he was driving out the thoughts in her head and replacing them with nothing but sensation.

Her body yielded until her chest sought his. Her breasts pushed against him. The tightness holding her heart—her lungs—captive eased. It was a heat that trickled down her spine. *And lower.*

She ached. *Everywhere.*

Her breathing changed. No longer was it short husks of too shallow air, but it was deep and full. Air he breathed between her lips, and she accepted it. Her body responded to it. It eased her tight muscles.

'Konstantinos,' she breathed into his mouth again.

She couldn't think. She could only feel. *Him.* The swipe of his tongue—the feel of his hand on the back of her neck holding her steady.

And then he was pulling away—abandoning her lips…

Her eyes opened. Her fingers clenched, tugging at his shirt—pulling him back.

Black eyes found hers.

She couldn't look away.

Her heart pulsed. It hadn't felt wrong to kiss him. It had felt like coming back to her own bed after too many nights away.

And her body had unfurled, leaned into every dip of the mattress that knew her body.

It was like…*coming home.*

'We are here,' he said, the breathy edge to his words the only sign he'd kissed her.

Her fingers unclenched. Her head snapped towards the window. Lights flashed from a sea of camera lenses. They couldn't see them behind the mirrored windows, but what had he been doing? Warming her up for the press?

He was not…*home.*

He was a bastard.

Tonight he'd done what he always had. She was honest—*open*—and he'd shut down any attempt to share in her vulnerability. His inability to talk had got them here. If he'd opened up to her about his feelings about the baby, shown his concern about the pregnancy not going well, if he'd shown her his own vulnerability, would she have hired the investigator?

It didn't matter.

She *had* hired them.

He hadn't been unfaithful to her with somebody else. But he *had* been unfaithful in all the ways that mattered to her. He hadn't been the person he'd promised to be. She hadn't been able to rely on him. He'd provided medical care, yes, but not his own presence. He'd left her alone to be treated by clinicians. But *they* didn't know what she'd lost. They couldn't understand her pain. But *he* should have.

She'd asked him to help—help her prepare for the arrival of their son, and he'd paid someone else to help her. And after, the funeral, he'd arranged it all, but he'd stayed away from her. Pulled his hand from hers when she held on. When she'd needed him to stay with her.

He should have been by her side.

'I hate you,' she said, because it was her armour and she would keep it.

He smiled. 'I know.' His thumb pressed beneath her lower lip, and he swiped. 'And we'll use it to our advantage.'

Her shoulders heaved. *'Advantage!'*

'The chemistry between us.' His hand fell. 'We'll show them nothing but *that*.' He held the evidence of their forbidden kiss between them: a red smudge covering the pad of his thumb. He reached for a tissue from his inside pocket and removed the proof of their kiss from his fingers—his mouth. 'This… *connection*.'

She wanted to deny it. Tell him whatever energy lingered in the air between them was all in his head.

It wasn't.

She bit at the inside of her cheek to stem the rage churning her insides that she'd gone so easily into his arms.

But no longer did Poppy think of the press outside.

No longer did the images of the articles she'd scoured play in her mind.

It was just…

His lips.

Konstantinos's gaze lingered on her mouth.

He may have wiped off the evidence of her mouth, but he could still taste the sweet tip of her tongue butting against his. The yield of her mouth as he pushed his tongue deeper. He knew, and so did she. The tight line of her mouth couldn't hide it. She could taste him still. Feel his hands on her.

'Stop looking at me like that,' she said, but her words lacked bite. Her voice was thick. Breathless.

'I am only looking.'

'But they're all going to be looking in a minute, I just… Aren't they waiting for us?'

'So eager to get out?'

She was eager, he recognised, and for that he was pleased.

She needed her hate, her anger towards him to be vibrant—
visceral—to get her out of the car and into the spotlight.

He'd done what needed to be done for them both. He'd kissed her—made her angry—so when she stepped out of this car her anger would give her strength.

She straightened her spine. 'I want to get this over with.'

She wanted to escape him.

His jaw locked.

His mind shifted him back to twelve months ago. Returning to Sotiría, carrying the weight of his father's death on his shoulders, and finding it empty. There had been no trace of her leaving. Her things. Clothes. Her passport. Everything was where she'd left it.

It was as if she'd just vanished.

If he hadn't been there to see his mother disappear into the sea, to the world she would have just vanished too. But Poppy, she had escaped. Escaped him. And...

Is that what his mother had tried to do? Escape his father?

He swallowed.

He'd done everything right. He hadn't locked her away and forgotten about her as his father had with his mother. He'd helped her. And still she'd run from him.

'Indeed,' he said, and turned his gaze away from her to the door.

He opened it to a flurry of activity. Lights flickered too brightly in his face. He turned away from them all. He didn't need to stop for questions. They only needed to see her alive to dispel the rumours. They only needed to know he hadn't failed her as he had his mother.

Poppy lived.

He walked to her door and opened it.

She stole his breath.

She was a vision in red silk.

He offered his hand. 'Shall we?'

Slowly, she slid her hand into his. He enclosed it.

The sweep of her eyes beneath diamond-dusted lashes rose from his hand to his face. And he knew the anticipation feathering her flesh, making her skin hum in his hand, was not fear of what was behind him. Not the press documenting their walk along the red carpet to the main entrance of the Palais Garnier.

She wasn't afraid of the dozens of black-suited security detail guarding the roads that were closed off for the night and blocked to the public. It was not the police on motorcycles barricading the steps to the metro.

It was the man holding her hand.

And she was right to be scared. Not of the press or their vindictiveness. But of him.

He pulled her to her feet. His hand slid to the naked dip of her spine. Her flesh shivered beneath his fingertips. He brought his head down low—brushing his lower lip against the lobe of her ear. 'Smile, *agape*.'

Each of her perfectly square white teeth appeared.

He moved the flat of his hand to her waist and ushered her body into the curve of his. He pulled her into step beside him, and she matched his slow ascent along the red carpet.

Eyes forward, they made their way to the entrance.

The green copper dome shimmered. Illuminated façades showcased the elaborate Beaux-Arts architecture, the ornate details of each statue, every twisted column standing tall…

The Palais Garnier, lit up against the night sky, was a beacon of beauty.

And there, at the central arcade, beside the two-winged sculptures keeping guard, Konstantinos stopped.

There, with everyone watching them, he turned her to face him.

Behind her was all of Paris, the buzz of questions shouted from paparazzi, and the roll of tyres as other selected invitees arrived. But her eyes only watched him, and he only looked at her.

Triumph, it teased at his lips.

She would do all he'd asked of her. She could have her contract in return. Everything she'd demanded last night he'd had outlined by his lawyer in detail. She could have Léon. She could have her divorce. The papers were already being prepared. There was to be no sex between them, but she'd skimmed over the sex part this morning with blushed cheeks.

Now it was written in black and white. She'd signed it with the slope of her elegant scrawl. As had he.

There was to be no penetrative sex, but *that* clause was to protect him. The protection they'd used was ninety-nine per cent effective, and it had failed them.

He wouldn't take that risk again.

He had no intention of her accidentally conceiving another child.

There would be no more accidents.

He'd abide by her every rule. He'd give her everything she'd asked for. *More.* Because his plan had grown legs—arms. And he understood the game afoot. He understood now how he'd get under her skin, how he'd remove her from under his, and claim back his control.

Konstantinos would seduce his wife.

He'd use the contract against her. Every rule she *hadn't* written. And when she craved him as she craved air—when she needed him—he'd send her away.

He lifted her hand, dipped his head, brought her fingers to his mouth, and feathered his lips across her knuckles.

He'd let her go.

He wouldn't look back.

He'd walk away.

Just as she had.

And what will you become without her? Will you fall back into your pit of despair?

His gut seized. The press had been right. Without her, searching for her, his world had been nothing but darkness.

He'd found her now.

He knew she was safe.

He'd restore order to his world.

There would be light without her.

CHAPTER SIX

'IF YOU PRESS this button...' the butler explained.

Poppy groaned inwardly. She didn't need to know a way to call Konstantinos back to the private box. *She* wouldn't be calling him. His were the last pair of eyes that would see her, at least for a little bit.

She needed a respite—*a moment to breathe*—without sly glances over the rims of champagne flutes.

The private showing tonight was an intimate affair. Twenty faces the public would recognise as masters in their individual fields, and swarm to buy their own tickets so they could see— *sit*—where the bottoms of the élite had graced.

She'd recognised a few faces from her life before. She'd lifted her smile higher, dipped her head. But tonight was not for talking. It was for being seen, not heard. And for that she was grateful. Grateful to the host who had ushered them through the Grand Foyer of a thousand stairs as champagne was thrust into their hands, all whilst a violin serenaded them with an intense sensual stroke of its strings and prepared them for what was to come.

The music had followed them into the auditorium of golden accents and red velvet. And, beneath the ceiling of vivid pinks and blues, she'd never felt more like an imposter.

She hadn't wanted to sit next to those people—to keep a smile that felt so plastic in place as she watched a show she knew she wouldn't see. She would only see those watching her. Feel their eyes on her, taking notes to feed the gossip that would be shared at every brunch tomorrow—every dinner table.

Never had her heart beat so fast in relief as Konstantinos led her by the elbow away from the masses as the others had taken their seats in the main gallery.

And now she was here, in their own private box.

There was no music serenading them now.

Only the pulse of her heart.

It hiccuped as the head of the butler turned, as he disappeared through the thick curtain, and it was only them.

Her smile fell.

'Sit,' he said, and as if she were a puppet, she did.

Her legs too stiff, her body too awkward, she sat down in the plush foam sheathed in the softest velvet. He sat beside her, stretched his long limbs…

The lights dimmed.

'You did well,' his voice hummed beside her too closely in the darkness.

She swallowed. 'I'm just glad it's over.'

'But it's not.'

His fingertips feathered her arm resting between them on the gold-leaf curl of their adjoining chairs.

'The press…' he said, the pad of his thumb swiping against the pulse thrumming in her bare wrist.

To anyone else, it was an innocent touch. No more than a husband touching his wife. A soothing gesture. But she wasn't anyone else. She was his soon-to-be ex-wife. And his touch did not soothe. It didn't feel innocent. It called to the nerves beneath her skin. It made them jump. *Pulse.*

'They'll still be outside when we leave,' he said.

She tensed.

Their red-carpet walk had been hell. She'd wanted to run. But she'd known she couldn't. And so, she'd matched his stride. A slow, purposeful walk that let everyone know he was in control. He didn't stop for questions. He didn't stop to the catcalls for a photo, or the intense cries of too many paparazzi asking in unison, *Where had she been?*

He didn't stop until he was ready. She'd followed him until he was. Until he'd taken her hand. *Kissed it.* And he'd let all those below them, clicking their long lenses as they stood on the wide steps, know that she was back.

She was *his.*

She wasn't.

No one was watching them now.

There was no one here to fool.

'Until we're back outside,' she said tightly. Slowly, *carefully*, Poppy reached for him in the darkness. She pressed her fingers into his wrist, her fingers barely enclosing its thickness. She lifted it. Moved it. Dropped it into his own lap. 'You can stop touching me.'

Her body rebelled. Because already her body missed it. The warmth of his fingers. The promise of them.

She curled her nails into her palms.

A piercing voice filled the auditorium. An operatic shrill that dug beneath her skin. The stage burst to life with figures dressed in fire reds and sunset oranges. And on their backs, broken black wings.

The full orchestra positioned beneath the stage flared to life, with every twist and turn of the ballet dancers on stage.

She'd been told tonight's performance would be different. A first for the Palais Garnier. A performance written and directed by an unknown who was a fast-rising star. *Their début.* It was a mash-up of classical allegro movements serenaded by the hum only a full orchestra could create with the modernist twist of hip-hop speech accompanied by an opera singer's voice.

It should have been too busy. Too many sounds. Too many different styles…

But it did something inside her.

It…*moved her*. But however much the colourful display on the stage held her eyes, the uniqueness of what she was seeing demanding it hold her attention…

His presence never faded.

He only watched *her*.

And his stare, it was too intense. *Too intimate*.

'You're missing it,' she husked.

'Am I?'

He didn't touch her again, but his eyes, they did. They swept over her. Made her aware of every inch of flesh exposed to the dip of his gaze. His eyes travelled down her throat, to her chest, rising too slowly.

Her traitorous body shivered.

'You're still tense,' he stated.

She didn't respond. Tension was threaded in her every muscle. It was bone-deep.

'I can help,' he offered.

'*Help?*' she mocked.

'I can give you what you need.'

Her stomach tensed. 'What I need?'

'You need to be touched, *agape*.' His voice was silk, but it scraped against her skin, waking every fine hair, and called them to stand.

'And I'm offering to give you release from the tension holding your shoulders too high, and your back too stiff. A reprieve from—' he swallowed heavily, and she almost felt it, the drag of his Adam's apple, the tension in his corded neck '—what is to come when the lights go back on.'

'No,' she said, because suddenly the darkness felt too tempting—*too inviting*. 'No, thank you.'

'I'm not offering you sex,' he clarified. 'I would, of course, not deviate from the contract. I would play safely within your carefully scripted rules.'

'How would you do *that*?'

'I would use my imagination, *glikia mou.*'

Hers ran riot. Of all the secret things he could do to her here. In the dark.

'No.'

'You need it,' he countered, his voice low. A whisper only her ears could hear. 'You need *me.*'

Her breath caught. Clarity formed—pushing the fog of illicit images in her mind apart to reveal a path of understanding at their centre.

It was a power play. *All of it.* The contract…

It had surprised her that he'd agreed to it, without correction, without changing the narrative he wanted the contract to fulfil other than the length of their agreement.

She could play within the lines, too.

Her heart racing, she reached for his hand. This time she didn't take it further away. She drew it nearer. Placed it in her own lap. On her stomach. And she knew he only needed a word, only her consent, and a new game would begin.

Hers.

'Okay.'

It was all Konstantinos needed to hear.

He'd been heavy-handed, but he was in no mood to be subtle. Watching her, watching the elaborate spectacle on the stage…

She hypnotised him.

The rise and fall of her chest, her small breasts straining against the bodice of her dress…

He hadn't been able to help himself. He wanted to stoke the flame in her eyes, play along with the music seeping into her ears. The fast pump of a song elevating her pulse, widening her eyes.

His fingers flexed on her stomach, firm and tense beneath his hand. She remained perfectly still. *Waiting.* Her hand on top of his. Trapping it against her. Her eyes remained on the stage, but he felt it. Her complete awareness of him. His eyes watching her.

He wanted her eyes.

He wanted *her to want him*.

He wanted her every thought to be about him as his thoughts had only been about her for the last year.

He'd been consumed by her.

By the thought of her out there, all alone.

Now she would be consumed by *him*.

Konstantinos moved. The pads of his fingers stroked over the silk clinging to the shape of her flat stomach like a second skin. The hand on top of his tensed. He stilled. Waited for her to throw his hand away—change her mind.

But she didn't.

She lifted her hand.

Freed his.

Gave him permission to roam, and fulfil his promise.

He looked out towards the stage. The audience below it.

He stiffened.

Casual scandal he couldn't allow.

He couldn't risk it. Poppy… She'd been through enough. *They both had*. Thanks to the paparazzi. But—he inhaled silently. *Deeply*. The scent of her trickled inside him. His nostrils flared.

Their private box was situated high on the left, behind the audience. Those down below couldn't see them. They would have to twist their necks, try to see beyond the column of marble obscuring them from their field of vision. Stand up and use binoculars.

They could do this.

If they were careful not to be heard.

He leaned in, moved his mouth to the sensitive patch of flesh beneath her ear.

'Can you be quiet, *agape*?' He breathed the question onto her skin.

'I can,' she confirmed, but he felt the strain in each word presenting itself in her too tight lips.

He knew how she liked to sing for him. How he caused her vocal cords to make sounds that were primal. *Primitive*. He wouldn't hear them tonight. She would be quiet. Keep her release a secret. But she would know who had given it to her. *Him*.

'And now?' Feather-light, he brushed his lips against her skin. 'Can you be quiet when I do this?' He applied pressure. Pressed his lips into her skin.

She shivered.

'Yes,' she said.

Slowly, he dragged his mouth down the taught tendons of her throat. He kissed it. *Licked it*. He sucked the flesh between neck and shoulder into his mouth. *Hard*.

'Oh!'

Compressed lips smothered her moan. But it fed him. Urged his fingers to stroke upwards, against the seam hiding the breasts straining for touch. *His touch*.

He teased her pebbled nipple.

'Konstantinos…'

His name was only a breath. *A whisper*.

He knew what it meant. What she wanted him to do. Where she wanted his hand to go next. But still, he stroked her nipple. Still, he teased with his fingers. His mouth.

And the tease was too much.

He wanted more.

His mind demanded it.

He lifted his head. Found her ear again. 'Did you miss this, *agape*?'

Hushed breath stuttered from her lips, but she didn't reply.

His hand abandoned her breast. It travelled downwards.

Stroking all that was in its path, until his fingers lingered where they could not touch—where they so desperately wanted to feel.

His length thrummed inside his trousers.

'Lift your skirt,' he commanded, keeping his voice lower than the music on stage. A demand only for her ears. But his voice, it was rough. *Wanton.*

This pleasure wasn't for him, he assured himself.

It was only to win.

Only to prove he was in control.

He lifted his head. The atmospheric light from the stage created a barely there light up here. Her skin was little more than of hues of grey. *Shadows.* In the semi-darkness he couldn't see his kiss. But he knew where it was. Where his mark would be.

He didn't care. Her shawl had fallen behind her. She could hide it if she wished. Or she could let them all see his brand. The only fact that was true. She would never know again when this was over—when he sent her away—*this* song.

Her hips lifted, and slowly she pulled up the silk hiding her from him.

Slowly, she revealed skin covered in sheer tights.

His hand dipped under the fabric of her skirt as she settled it on her thighs. The fabric that would hide his exploration. Keep it secret.

They were not tights.

They were stockings.

His blood roared as he explored the seam of her panties. As he touched the exposed softness of her inner thigh.

'*Please*,' she whispered.

His entire body swelled.

His victory—*so close*—his for the taking.

He took it.

He swiped his fingers up and down the seam. He stroked the intimate heart of her. Until her breathing was so fast—*so deep*—he knew it was time. Time to give her what he'd promised.

He swept her panties aside. He didn't tease. He didn't caress. He pushed his fingers inside her. And she kept her word. The scream in her mouth. She held it in. But he felt it. The tight grip of its roar holding her flesh captive.

His thumb encircling her engorged nub, he drove into her, curled his fingers. Her intimate muscles squeezed around him. His every thrust, she dragged him deeper. Raised her hips a little. Pushed them down.

He moved with her. Listened to her trapped moans getting faster, and faster, until he knew she was coming.

He pushed, found the secret tangle of muscles inside her.

And he held her there.

Her eyes closed. *Tightly.*

'Come, *agape*,' he commanded, because she was there. All she needed to do was take what his fingers were giving her—commanding *she* give to him.

'*Konstantinos!*' It was a choked breath. A fierce whisper after no more than a gulp of air. But it was a scream to his ears.

It was surrender.

It was victory.

Her eyes opened. She didn't look at him. She looked to the hand still between her thighs—at the fingers still inside her. She reached for him. Withdrew him. His fingers wanted to push against her—find her again. *Do it all again.* And he knew all she had to do was ask.

He wanted her to ask.

And she would.

He did nothing. He let her hold his hand. Gave her the illusion she was in control of what happened next. What pleasure he'd give to her next.

'Thank you,' she said, and she moved, dropped his hand

onto his lap, onto the too hard part of himself that did not want his own hand.

It wanted her mouth.

A gift she had offered once before. To take him between her lips. To kiss him. But it had felt too much like surrender. It made him feel…*vulnerable*. In *her* power. Her control. And he had not wanted *that*. To lose himself between her lips. For her to control…*him*. So he had not encouraged it. He'd stopped it.

He did not need *that* kiss from her.

Slowly, she folded down her skirt. Placed her own hands in her lap and knotted her fingers.

She didn't look at him.

She looked only to the stage. To the singers now too loud in his ears. Their song was a screech. It made his temples throb.

He turned his head to the stage—to see what held her gaze. It was an explosion of colour now.

His head snapped back to her.

She was in complete control of herself.

He wanted her listless in his arms. *Overwhelmed.*

But she wasn't.

'We are leaving.'

'Why?' she asked quietly. And only then did she turn to him. Her eyes…they blazed. Her hand moved. Her fingers stroked the inside of his thigh. And they rose higher. 'Don't you want to test how quiet you can be, Konstantinos?'

His blood roared.

She smiled.

His heart stuttered.

'I will not deviate from the rules,' she promised.

Just as *he* had.

His eyes blew wide.

She was outmanoeuvring him? Playing him at his own game?

He—

'I can help ease the tension from your too tight shoulders,

Konstantinos.' Her hand moved to the centre of his thighs. 'You need to be touched,' softly, she teased him. Her fingertips crept up along the seam of his zip. 'By *me*.'

The reversal of his seduction. It turned him on. *Outraged him*. In equal parts.

Once he'd enjoyed her ability to say his words back to him after she'd taken minutes in a meeting, echoing his choices for his employees, or his business. She'd made him hear his words—*his choices*—differently. Hear what was missing.

He'd found it attractive. *Once*.

He didn't find the echo of his words attractive now.

His words on her lips sounded…*cold*.

He caught her wrist. 'I do not need anything.'

Or anyone, he added silently.

He released her wrist as if it were a burning ember.

His every muscle was too tight. *Twisted*.

He wouldn't let her see how much she affected him. *Still*.

He stood.

'We are leaving. *Now*.'

CHAPTER SEVEN

Five Days Later...

PARIS BUZZED WITH an undercurrent of activity. Lights flickered on every street. The Eiffel Tower blazed in its night-time illuminated splendour.

Poppy reached for her hot chocolate, held it between her palms, and sipped.

She should be frantic—*worried*.

Tonight was the Versailles Masked Ball, and she wasn't ready. She wasn't dressed. She sat on the wraparound balcony of Konstantinos's penthouse Parisian home, in her fluffy white towelling robe, and her flannel PJs.

Tonight, the PR façade would be back in play for all to see. They would appear united. A team.

They were not united. He didn't want to talk. He hadn't in the car. He hadn't before. But she needed to. She needed to talk to him. *Tonight*. Before they went back into the spotlight.

She'd upset Konstantinos, she knew, but she'd upset herself, too.

She *was* upset.

Everything had been moving so fast, from being on the run, to capture, to her imprisonment. She hadn't had a moment to breathe. *To think*. She'd just reacted. *Responded*. To him.

The last few days without him... He'd avoided her. Tangled himself in immovable meetings. *Supposedly*. But she understood what he was doing. It would be easy for her to do it. Distract herself from what had happened. *What was happening.* But she *had* thought about it. She'd made herself think. Analyse her every decision.

Control. *That* night at the ballet, they'd both demanded it, locked behind their walls, guarded by the impenetrable need to win it from the other. But their marriage was over. There was no winning. There was no going back. They needed to be adults about this, and…*talk.*

'Why aren't you dressed?'

She turned, and there he stood. His navy-blue tie wrenched free from his throat, exposing the four undone buttons of his crumpled white shirt.

'Why aren't *you*?' she countered.

'I'm not dressed,' he said, stepping onto the balcony, 'because I was informed you'd sent the team of stylists away, and were sitting in your pyjamas out here, staring into the void.'

'I wasn't ready for them.'

'And is the reason you're not ready out there?' he asked, waving to the sky. 'What exactly are you waiting for?'

She swallowed. 'You.'

His nostrils flared. 'Me?'

'We need to talk.'

His gaze flicked to the silver face of the watch on his wrist. 'There is no time to talk.'

Her eyes travelled over the tightness in his shoulders, making them appear broader—*bigger.*

'We need to *make* time.'

He stepped closer. 'And what is it you wish to speak about?' His voice snapped sharply like a thwacked belt. 'Do you want to tell me I'm an unfaithful bastard again? Do you want to tell me how much you hate me? Do you want to talk about Isabella?'

'Why would I want to talk about *her*?'

'Because she is the woman you believe I was unfaithful

with.' His whole body radiated with a barely contained energy. 'And are you now sick to your stomach, Poppy, that you let me put my treacherous fingers on your body?' He took a step closer. 'Does it make you ill? How such a cruel man, a lying *bastard*, could make you come so sweetly?'

'I…' she almost choked. So consumed had she been by protecting herself. Safeguarding herself with contracts and rules… She'd thought it, but she hadn't told him she believed him.

'I know you weren't unfaithful.'

'You know—' his face twisted '—*what?*'

'Isabella—she's your PA—'

'*Was*,' he corrected. 'I let her go the day my father died.'

He'd let her go? She shook it off. It didn't matter.

'You were working together…' she continued, picking up her train of thought. 'She may have wanted you—who doesn't want you?'

'My wife,' he countered too quickly.

Her throat constricted. She *did* want him. Physically, at least.

'I know you pushed her away… I believe you.'

He didn't reply, but his eyes were shuttered.

There was just…*nothing*.

'I'm sorry about your dad, Konstantinos. I'm sorry he died and—'

'I do not need your condolences,' he said, his voice flat. 'I require you to get dressed.'

'I will.' She swallowed. Her body was too tight. *Too conflicted*. This wasn't how she'd imagined this conversation would go. She didn't want it to be like *this*. 'After you tell me how long he was sick for.'

'My father?'

Neck stiff, she nodded.

'What does it matter?'

'I want to know.'

'Months. Pancreatic cancer.'

'I'm so sorry,' she breathed, because she was. 'I know you hated him,' she said, because they both hated their fathers… this she knew.

They hadn't swapped stories of trauma before bed, but they knew the facts that mattered to each other. The bits that had brokered the terms of their marriage. She understood his relationship was complicated with his father. So was hers. Her father was unfaithful. His was a cruel tyrant. But still, she'd grieved for her father.

'Why didn't you tell me?' she asked quietly, because she needed to know—to understand why he kept a secret from her he hadn't needed to.

His jaw firmed to a shadowed line. 'Your behaviour— you were sick. You didn't need to know. What would it have achieved to tell you a man you cared nothing for was dying? I needed closure from his death. *You* would have gained nothing from the knowledge of his passing.'

'Did you get it?' she asked. 'Closure?'

He shook his head. A single swipe.

She sighed. Whatever his reasons were for not telling her about his father, he had no justifiable excuse for withdrawing from her over Isaak's death. His decision to do *that*, it would hurt her for ever.

'Were you ever going to tell me he was ill?'

He stared at her. His gaze was empty. *Vacant.* But for the first time, Poppy noticed the bruises beneath his eyes.

'The day he died,' he said flatly, 'I was going to tell you about my father, but you'd vanished.'

His words were a knife in her chest.

He'd needed her, and she hadn't tried to talk to him.

She hadn't tried to communicate with him at all.

She'd left him all alone.

He'd had no one.

She was no better than Konstantinos, was she?

She was to blame for the end of their marriage as much as he was.

He turned on his heel.

'Get dressed, Poppy.'

The string quartet's song echoed from the high vaulted ceilings. It kept time with the clink of glasses and complemented the hum of conversations spoken from painted lips to ears. Discussions that only happened in private where deals were brokered with champagne and music.

Conversations Konstantinos hadn't been a part of for too long.

He understood tonight was the perfect way to reintroduce himself into rooms he hadn't wanted to grace without her.

Tonight the press was locked out.

The tall golden gates had closed behind them and shut them out.

This ball was only for the élite. *A secret event.*

There were two yearly masquerade balls at the palace. One was for the public, with tiered tickets. *This* ball did not have tiers. It did not have tickets printed from black and white machines, but invitations delivered by white-gloved hands in black velvet envelopes with the words written in gold silk.

He should pay attention.

He was present, but he wasn't *here*.

What had happened on the balcony. Her confession. She believed him. It had shaken him. He was still shaken, because he didn't know what it meant. She trusted he'd kept his vows, and yet everything was still the same.

She was still leaving him.

Do you want her to stay?

He repressed the growl building in his chest.

He wanted her to *want* to stay. To admit she was wrong. To admit he hadn't broken his promise to be faithful. To be the man she could rely on. He wanted her to regret her decision to leave. Regret the day she'd turned her back on him.

You couldn't protect her or Isaak. Why would she regret walking away from a man who couldn't protect his family?

He'd done all he could.

She was alive.

Konstantinos understood he shouldn't stand here alone.

He should '*work*' the room. But he looked at only her.

She was faultless. *Perfection.* And she blinded him to the sea of bodies surrounding her.

She sparkled beneath the teardrop-diamond chandeliers. Her throat was bare, his mark healed, or concealed, he didn't know.

A cape, intricately embellished with sequins and crystals, guarded her silhouette from the pointed flourishes at her shoulders to sweep to the floor to meet the spike of a gold heel. The gold sequinned gown beneath accentuated every line. Every dip of her body.

It was silk, gold armour.

He was too far away to hear what she was saying, but he watched her lips move. Unpainted, they glistened with the sheer shine of the moisture from the tip of her pink tongue. He watched it disappear. Her lips meet. He watched her head lift. *Turn.* And behind her sequinned mask, her eyes met his.

All night, she'd done her duty. Kept *her* promise.

She'd worked the room. Danced. Talked. *Smiled.*

She did not smile now.

The current between them pulsed too strongly. *Too heavily.*

It was magnetic. The drag, urging him closer.

Like in London?

No. In London it had been an explosion of repressed desire. *Now?* He desired his wife. He wanted her, just as desperately. Just as viscerally. But it wasn't like their first time together.

He'd never intended to take her to bed in London. He'd never intended to keep her in it until they both came up for air, exhilarated. *Exhausted.* Only to do it again. And again, because as soon as she'd agreed to an affair—agreed to let him taste the body he'd coveted for months—he'd lost the fight to stay away from her.

But *this* was…*different.*

A desire intensified by time—by knowing her more intimately than he knew himself.

Their desire…trust intensified it. It always had. They understood in this room full of strangers: they had each other. And they knew they had each other's back.

He was conflicted by *that* truth.

She made him conflicted. She hadn't needed proof of his fidelity. She'd taken him at his word and needed nothing else. And yet she needed her contract. Her divorce.

Konstantinos longed to tear his eyes from hers. To feign indifference. But he couldn't.

Relief eased his shoulders as her eyes dipped back to the companion at her side. A blur of purple beside her. Her white teeth appeared from behind lifting lips. She nodded. Moved. Claimed two glasses of champagne from a passing server. She walked beneath frescos painted on the vaulted ceilings. The dangling lights of chandeliers guided her with every footfall.

The hall of mirrors created an optical feast of light.

It made *her* image endless.

She stood in front of him. Handed him a glass of champagne. He reached for it. They paused. Their hands aloft. Their fingers met.

It burnt.

'The fireworks are about to begin.' He nodded towards the black-waistcoated hosts, handing gold-cupped candles to gloved hands beside the exit at the end of the hall. 'We should make our way outside,' he said, because her scent… It was everywhere. He needed air. He needed out. He needed to put space and people between them.

'Let's drink our champagne first.' She took a slow, controlled sip. 'I'm sorry.'

'For what?'

'I'm sorry you thought you couldn't tell me about your father.'

'I do not need your apologies, *glikia mou*,' he dismissed with a flick of his wrist. But his chest. It spasmed. At her proximity. Her sincerity.

For days, Konstantinos had kept his distance. Locked himself in his world of boats and business. He'd kept away from her because he'd wanted her to pine—*to yearn*. He'd been waiting for something. A call, a text to tell him she needed more than his hands. His fingers. She needed *him*. But she hadn't called. She had not texted. His team had. They'd told him. There she sat, all alone, despondent, looking out at a view with eyes that did not look. Did not see.

He'd seen her this way too many times. He'd watched her from the doorway of too many rooms when she'd refused to speak, to get dressed.

He'd watched his mother do the same. Refuse to eat, talk—get dressed. He'd gone to his mother and sat at her knee. Waited for her to see him. She never had. No matter what he said—how many times he tried to hold her.

Physical comfort was nothing but a physical display of emotion that helped no one.

Physical comfort would not have helped Poppy. She'd needed the professionals his mother hadn't had. She had not needed his arms.

But he didn't want to see Poppy like *that* again. *Lost*.

But when he'd seen her tonight… She was…*calm*. At peace. So different from the Poppy he'd been confronted with every day after Isaak's death.

She wasn't sad any more.

She wasn't lost to despair.

She was not like his mother. She had felt her feelings and dealt with them. She had not been consumed by them. They had not killed her.

His eyes travelled over her mask. Her face was in two halves. One half was made of hard gold and crystals, the other… His eyes lingered on her mouth. So soft. *So vulnerable.* Had she always had two halves? Yes, she was vulnerable—*soft*—but so strong was she, to have felt her grief—mourned so hard—and yet here she was. *Fighting.*

'But I'm sorr—'

'Do not apologise again.' Konstantinos placed his glass down on a nearby table. 'I don't want or need it. We are here. The night is almost over. Tonight was a success. *That* is all that matters.' He moved towards the few remaining people leaving.

Fingers, featherlight, caught his wrist.

She shook her head, her eyes flicking to the hosts gathering everyone still lingering, and leading them out into the garden for the night's finale.

She put her finger to her lips. Her hand moved. Her fingers speared between his, and led him through the arched exit behind them.

And he let her lead him into the dark.

A windowless antechamber.

Her breath quickened as did his.

'Stay quiet,' she whispered.

'Why are we hiding?' he whispered back.

She held a finger to her lips.

Curiosity assaulted him, so he played along.

He didn't speak again, nor did she.

They listened.

The baroque music from the string quartet faded in the adjoining room.

The lights dimmed.

And in the dark, he stayed hidden with *her.*

Konstantinos waited for her to tell him why she wanted to hide with *him*, because it didn't feel sexual. It did not feel like a promise of the delights the dark could give them.

They stood, side by side, in a darkened corner, going nowhere.

And somehow...

It felt like escape.

CHAPTER EIGHT

POPPY UNTHREADED HER FINGERS, and pulled her hand free from the palm of his.

'I think they're gone,' she said into the silence, and moved in front of him.

He wore all black. Tiny silver accents were everywhere. On the cuffs of his shirt. They created the buttonholes, lined every seam of his costume…

He looked like an angel kissed by stardust.

'And why did you want them gone?' he asked. 'Why are *we* not with them?'

'You didn't want to be with them.' She searched the dark depths of his eyes behind his mask.

It was a simple design. Black silk with silver swirls sewn in delicate detail around his eyes. It covered his sculpted cheekbones, his noble nose, but it didn't hide his eyes, his mouth.

His lips thinned. 'What made you believe *that*?'

'Because neither did I.'

She turned on her heel and walked back into the hall of mirrors. The lights had been turned off, but the hue from the palace gardens lit the space. It reflected from the wall of glass to her left.

'And so because you wanted to stay behind,' he said, his following footfall silent behind her, 'you thought *I* did too?'

She stopped beneath the first tall columns. The window between them was an array of squares, each locking in a different flush of green from the palace gardens. 'Yes.'

He stood beside her. 'But how did you know?'

She tilted her head—looked up at him. 'Was I wrong?'

'How did you know?' he pressed, his question an urgent husk.

'Little things.'

He frowned. 'Little things?'

'The tension in your shoulders,' she said, her eyes following the rigid length of his broadness. 'The flick of the pulse in your throat.'

And it pulsed now under her gaze. *Hard.*

'I'm not tense,' he denied.

'I knew, because we're married,' she said. 'Because I noticed you didn't hurry to leave—that we stayed back.'

'No.' His black eyes flashed with a thousand shards of silver ice. 'You're a creature of too many contradictions, Poppy. *You* called me a stranger. You can't bend your convictions to suit you, because *you* want the night to end before it's over. We'll go outside. *Now.*'

He turned to leave, but gently she placed her fingers to his arm. Halted him.

All night she'd played the dutiful wife. Ignored the barbs of curiosity asking questions laced in venom, to acquire knowledge of her life—*her marriage*—for their titillation. And she'd done it for him. But this she would do for herself.

'We've done enough for tonight,' she said, because they had.

But had *she* done enough?

Her heart shrank. It had been easy to see his lack of desire to join the others. Little things anyone who knew him even a little could have seen, if only they'd looked.

She hadn't been looking before.

She hadn't noticed.

Guilt bloomed, thick and heavy, in her throat.

Silent boom, after silent boom, the fireworks illuminated the space. Highlighted each one of his dark, slashing features.

He dipped his head. 'Did you want to stay behind for this?' His heated breath feathered her lips.

'For what?'

'*This*.' He claimed her mouth. Konstantinos possessed it. Commanded it with the skilful pressure of his to open. To let him in. His hands went to her waist She stepped with him as he pulled them from the view of the window to the columned wall beside it.

Her hands rose to his arms. They bulged in her grasp. Strength. *Power.* It was laced in every muscle throbbing beneath her touch. And she knew she should yank his arms away. That she should not open for him. She shouldn't let his tongue sweep between her lips and thrust inside.

But she did.

She kissed him just as fervently.

He dragged his mouth from hers. And both breathless, both panting, they stared at each other.

'*More*,' she husked.

He fell to his knees. Hid his gaze in the folds of her dress. His hands gripped her hips. He placed hard, fervent kisses to her stomach.

He reached for the gold hem of her dress at her feet.

She steadied herself on the arc of his shoulders.

'Tell me *this* is the more you want,' he commanded. But his fingers stilled. The dress barely exposing the naked flesh of her ankles held in his waiting fingers.

She closed her eyes. Tried to stem the melting urgency of her body.

She wanted him to lift her skirts higher.

Their desire… Still, it rampaged through her. Stronger than it ever had been. And she knew why. It was because on the balcony she'd glimpsed something.

Something vulnerable beneath his suit.

He'd never reacted to the death of their son with anything resembling the pain she hadn't been able to contain. But in those articles… Those images… On the balcony tonight…

It was armour, wasn't it? His image. His public reputation.

On the balcony, it had cracked. She wanted to know who lived inside. To see him break loose from his rigid demeanour of self-control. From the rules that had guided them in their marriage to always put his image first. To keep the fire between them to the bedroom. Behind closed doors.

She wanted to see him as desperate as she was.

She wanted him to surrender to these emotions driving through them here. *Now.*

And if he can? What does that prove?

He was human.

He…*felt.*

And if he felt, he could grieve and maybe, just maybe, he felt something for their son.

'It is,' she said, and braced herself. Her skirts rose. His mouth pressed hard little kisses to her calf, her knee, her inner thigh.

Then he was there.

At the heart of her.

'Poppy,' he breathed against her skin.

She tingled. *Everywhere.* Anticipation dimming out everything but the need to have his mouth closer.

Konstantinos gripped her hips—pulled his mouth harder against her.

Her fingers cradled his scalp. '*Yes,*' she moaned.

His tongue lathed up and down her panties on top of her intimate folds.

Poppy let out a helpless whimper.

The sky outside exploded in Technicolor. Every mirrored surface in front of her flared into a rainbow of light. And then she saw *them* contained within the mirrored display. Bursts of light bringing their shadowed bodies out of the darkness.

It was erotic. It was—

His mouth clamped around her throbbing nub. He sucked. Kissed her. *Deeply.*

'Konstantinos!'

The fireworks outside were inside her now. Continuously. *Breathlessly.* They exploded.

Konstantinos stood, and drew her in against him. Held her as her body pulsed. She leaned into him. Placed her head on his chest and breathed.

Clarity formed in the fog of pleasure, softening her body against his.

He'd always taken charge of the conversation in and out of bed. What if *she* did? What if she took charge in a way he'd never allowed?

She'd tried. *Once.* But he'd stopped her…

Poppy fell to her knees.

Konstantinos watched her fall.

His solar plexus shifted into a roll of tremors.

The wall at her back, they couldn't be seen.

Poppy on her knees before him.

It should feel like a gift. *A victory.* But he couldn't breathe deeply enough.

Her eyes locked onto her intended task. Her small hands reached for him. His hips. Her fingers feathered over the arch of them. Feathered inwards over the leather of his belt and stilled at the silver buckle.

Her eyelashes fell.

Her head dipped.

The roll of his flesh intensified.

She kissed him on his stomach. Beneath his belly button. Her fingers reached for the buckle of his belt. She undid it with trembling fingers until it was released. She reached for the button. Undid that too. Pulled down his zip. And her kiss, it travelled down. Over the black fabric covering the swell of him. *The hardness.*

He pulsed beneath her lips. He ached for the barrier between them to disappear. But she didn't rush to pull his trousers down, or his boxers. She pressed small, experimental kisses to his straining erection.

He closed his eyes—curled his fingers into tight fists at his sides.

He refused to do what his body demanded. He wouldn't free himself. Arch forward. Claim the heat of her promised kiss.

He didn't open his eyes as her head lifted, removing the pressure. But the ache inside him didn't ease. It intensified as he felt her fingers fumble with the tiny black buttons on the front of his boxers. As her fingers teased inside. And she found him. *Touched him.*

He shuddered.

This was winning, wasn't it?

This was taking back his control.

This was one step closer to his end goal.

She wanted him, despite her contract. She was playing inside her own rules because *he* had made her want to. He'd made her believe she was safe inside the boundaries of them.

So why did it feel like he wasn't in control? But *she* was? Why did his knees feel weak? Why did his feet not feel planted? Why did it feel as though he wasn't exorcising her from beneath his skin, but as if he was allowing her deeper? *Into his bones?*

This was not what he wanted.

He was almost blind with need.

He was hanging on to control with his fingernails.

His bones locked.

He turned rigid.

He hauled her up by her arms. Yanked her into his heaving chest.

'What is it?' she asked breathlessly. Her fingers reached for the granite firmness of his gritted jaw.

He speared his fingers into her hair—watched the tendrils come loose from the knot at her nape, and fall to her shoulders. Her gaze clung to his. Her eyes so blue—*so wide*—so tempting. The urge was bone-deep to dip his head. Taste her.

He would control himself.

He would stop this. *Now.*

She brushed her lips over his.

'Poppy,' he warned.

'Konstantinos,' she replied, her hands reaching between them.

She freed him. Stroked him. *Intimately.* Until she held him—enclosed him.

He pulsed in her palm.

His control shattered.

He backed her into the wall. Her soft kiss changed. She pressed her mouth harder against his. Her tongue a darting arrow, it drove inside him. Demanded he feel only *that*. Only her tongue. *Only her.*

'*Ahh*,' he groaned.

It was too much pleasure. Too painful. Too…*everything*.

Everything he'd missed. *Her.*

Her legs parted, accommodating the pressure of his hips. 'I need you inside me, Konstantinos. *Now.*'

Her need. It made him swell.

This was what he wanted. Her complete surrender. But it didn't feel like a win. It only felt…*right*. Right to be here. Between her legs. His body only millimetres from being sheathed where he'd yearned to be for so long. Inside her.

His fingers pinched the fabric at her hips, scrunched it tightly into his fists as it rose up her legs.

'*Theos mou…*'

She shifted, placing her high-heeled foot against his lower back. His arms went beneath her firm bottom. Supported her. Lifted her. The heat of him pressed against her core.

'*Please*,' she mewed into his mouth.

He arched his hips. Pressed himself into her heat. The barrier of her panties gave way, but it didn't give him what he wanted. To thrust up inside her and find oblivion.

He dragged his mouth from hers, buried his face in the crook of her throat. He moved his hips. The heat of him leapt between them. He trapped it against her stomach.

'Konstantinos?'

'I don't have any protection.'

'I'm on the pill.'

It was a bitter-sweet temptation.

The swell of him pulsed on the flat of her stomach.

'It's not enough. The pill failed us before.'

'A rarity,' she assured him, but he wasn't assured.

He knew what could happen.

He remembered what they'd lost because it had failed them.

'It's too much of a risk,' he roared against her flesh in a muffled cry of defeat.

He hadn't been careful enough with her in the past.

So safe had he thought they were, in their marriage, in the world they'd built together.

He'd thought nothing could burst the bubble around them. But *he* had got her pregnant.

It was his fault. *All of it.*

He'd turned their world upside down.

He hadn't protected her from…*the accident.*

It tore through him.

Something sharp.

Something foreign.

'No,' he growled.

He'd *almost* failed her again.

Failed himself.

'We must stop. *Now.*'

'*Please*,' she said. 'It's extremely unlikely the contraceptive would fail us twice.'

'No.' He lowered her leg to the floor. Pulled himself free of her embrace. Turned his back on her and walked towards the exit whilst he did up his zip. His belt. He stopped walking. Waited for her.

Her heels clicked over the floor as she moved to join him. She stood beside him. Her spine was straight. Her shoulders squared. Her feet planted.

It was a fighting stance that mirrored his own.

Konstantinos understood that tonight he'd lost the battle between them.

He *was* weak.

All the control had firmly been in her hands right until *he'd* ended it. The risk was too great for them both. But if he'd had a condom. If he'd been able to double their protection. Reduce the risk…

He needed time to reinforce his self-control.

'You'll go home,' he said. 'To Greece.'

Her brow lifted. 'Only me?'

'You must…'

His jaw gritted.

He needed—

'I need some time,' he admitted truthfully, his voice hoarse. 'Away from you.'

CHAPTER NINE

One Week Later...

POPPY TOOK THE plastic tip of the pin out of her mouth and pushed it through the purple petal. She stuck it onto Table 26. That table would be purple-themed. Delicate hues to complement the stark russet orange of Table 25 at the reception after they'd renewed their vows.

Konstantinos had hired a team to organise the ceremony.

She'd taken over the planning.

She needed *this*.

Something to focus on.

Something to take her mind off…*him*.

She took a step back. Stared at the table arrangements. She'd taken over the lounge. Presentation boards, three of them, stood at the centre of the arched floor-to-ceiling window. Papers were scattered on the wooden floor beneath them.

She'd missed *this*. Organising things. Mapping events to bring people's lives together seamlessly. She'd been good at it. Her job. And that was how she was trying to look on the ceremony. As an event. An abstract thing where she wouldn't be the focal point, and neither would he.

She hadn't missed working for so long. Still didn't. Not really. She knew this was a distraction at best. But so far, the distraction wasn't working.

She knew what he'd done at Versailles. She'd done it. So many times.

He'd run away.

She took another flower and pinned it with a forceful jab into Table 27.

She hadn't missed working when she'd married Konstantinos. She'd given up her job with ease the minute she'd accepted his proposal. Being a wife—*his wife*—she'd enjoyed it. All of it. The clothes, the jewellery, the social engagements, the business dinners, or intimate meals with CEOs and their wives, where she hadn't had to take notes, or arrange a docket of who was attending to inform Konstantinos what he should know about their personal lives—the birth of a grandchild, or the death of a cousin.

She'd slipped into her new role, she knew, because of him.

He'd held her hand and led her into the spotlight of his life, and never had she felt as if she didn't belong there. As if she wasn't wanted. As if she was someone to be kept a secret. In the dark.

She'd never known if her father wanted her or *them*. Which family was his family? Both or neither? Was *she* the dirty secret he kept away from her siblings—from their mother? Which one of his families had been the mistake? Had he cared for any of them? Had they all been unwanted by her father so he could live his carefree life regardless of who he hurt? Had he ever wanted her?

Konstantinos had wanted her. He'd needed her to secure the honourable life he wanted to lead.

She'd found strength in their relationship.

A safe marriage where no one could get hurt.

A successful relationship, measured by respect, trust, and safety. *Rules.*

Isaak had shaken the foundations of their marriage.

Obliterated their every rule. Smashed the agreed-upon foundations they'd thought were so very strong. *She had.* But… after… The extravagance of her life—the financial safety of it—what Konstantinos provided…

It was a hollow thing after Isaak's death. *Empty.* A lonely place. Superficial.

Everything she'd thought she needed to feel safe had meant nothing in the face of her loss. The pain. Nothing had felt safe. But she'd never asked Konstantinos for what she needed. *Him.* She'd expected him to be there. To *want* to be there for her. *He* hadn't. But she'd never said those words. Never told him she needed *him.* Not with words.

She'd stopped being honest with him the minute they'd conceived their baby. She hadn't been ready to be vulnerable. Not on purpose. Not by choice. When she was sick she *had* been vulnerable. *Exposed.* It hadn't been a choice.

And it had revealed how weak their relationship was. Their marriage, it wasn't strong. It couldn't withstand the unexpected harshness of reality, because what held them together, sex, and conversations that never went beneath the surface, it didn't make them friends. Not *real* friends. And that was why they hadn't survived. The rules they'd bound themselves to had pushed them apart.

At Versailles, he'd shut down. Removed himself from the conflict brewing between them. Just as *she* had a year ago. Just as *he* had when she was sick. When Isaak had died…

He'd looked away from her distress, and she'd looked away from his.

They couldn't carry on like this.

They needed to talk about the divide between them. Address what lived inside it.

Isaak.

Wood creaked.

Poppy turned towards the doors.

The gold handles moved. *Downwards*. The doors opened inwards.

His gaze narrowed, moved over her cut-off denim shorts, her bare legs, unpainted toes, and flicked to her boards.

'How's the planning going?'

Her heart raced. 'I don't want to talk about the ceremony.'

He stepped into the room, and with a graceful flick of his white-cuffed wrist Konstantinos closed the doors behind him. 'Why not?'

'I want to talk about what happened at Versailles.'

He shook his head. A graceful swipe. 'It won't happen again.'

'Nothing happened,' she corrected. '*You* didn't let it happen.'

'But you wished it did?' He stalked closer. 'You wish something happened between us?' he asked, his eyes holding hers fast. 'You no longer wish to enforce it, Poppy?' He stood in front of her. Six-feet-plus of nothing but tight, defined muscle standing before her. His black suit moulded to his muscular frame. 'The contract?'

The contract had left her wide open. She'd tried to protect herself with her no-sex clause. He'd turned it into a weapon to win control. She'd retaliated.

There would never be closure, unless they both did what had to be done.

'No, I don't,' she admitted tightly.

'You wish to have sex?'

Her mouth ran dry. She wasn't prepared. For the smell of him. A cologne both bitter and sweet. A scent her body responded to. Her pupils widened. Her nostrils flared. Heat arrowed to her pelvis.

She swallowed. 'I don't know,' she admitted. At Versailles she'd wanted him. She wanted him. *Still*. But sex…it wasn't what they needed. *Not now.*

His eyes blazed. 'If not for sex, why do you no longer wish to enforce the contract?'

'We need to forgive each other. We need to heal, Konstantinos,' she told him on a breath. 'We need…*closure*. But we
can't have any of those things,' she continued, 'if we keep doing
what we always do.'

'What we always do?' he repeated.

'Start conversations and end them in bed.'

'We haven't slept in a bed together for longer than I can remember.'

'If we take *this* conversation to bed—our marriage, even
after the divorce, will be…*unresolved*. We owe each other—'
she held her hands up wide, palms forward '—more than *this*.
More than a contract that divides us further. Because if we
keep it up, this power play for control, someone will lose. And
haven't we lost enough already?'

He flinched. An almost imperceptible jump of his flesh. But
she saw it. *Felt it*.

Her lips grappled with the air. 'I still want a divorce, Konstantinos,' she said. 'Too much has happened for us to do anything else. But I want to trust that you'll give one to me, without
a contract.'

His jaw clenched. '*Why?* It will change nothing.'

'I… I should have trusted you to do the right thing. I… I
lost my head at the ball, but *you* kept yours,' she reminded him.
'You kept your word, even though I didn't want you to.' She
bit her lip. 'I trust you, Konstantinos. I want *you* to trust I'll do
everything you have asked me to do. We always trusted each
other before everything…*imploded*.'

His pupils flared, until there was nothing but black rings of
intensity holding her captive.

'What exactly do you want from me, *agape*?'

Her command to her lungs to breathe slowly, *deeply*, dis-
obeyed her.

Confrontation, *still*, it made her heart pump, her stomach
twist, but this was the only way.

He'd abandoned her on a private jet after Versailles. Abandoned her. Sent her back to Greece. Alone. To be guarded by a team of strangers. Security that patrolled the island's borders. Staff to feed her. Clean up after her. Just as she had been living for weeks—*months*—before and after the funeral.

She wanted to show him she wasn't the wife he'd married. She wouldn't be amenable. Compliant to the rules that no longer served him or her. She wasn't *her* any more. The woman he could leave on the other side of the monastery all alone.

She was here.

He was here.

She wanted—*needed*—to have the conversations they hadn't.

She wouldn't leave their marriage open. *Unresolved.*

She needed closure.

'I want to talk about what happened at the ball,' she repeated. 'I want to talk about why you left. Why you needed to get away from me.'

'You know why,' he growled.

She walked past him—broke the too tense pull between them. She sat down on the sofa, pressed her knees together, and looked up at him from her seated position.

If she wanted him to talk, she had to lead by example. She had to let herself be open to change. She had to let herself be vulnerable. Nothing would ever be different between them unless *she* did things differently. If things never changed, she'd never have closure.

'I do,' she agreed. 'And we need to talk about it.'

She dragged in a fortifying breath.

'We need to talk about Isaak.'

'He's gone, Poppy.' He gritted his teeth to stem the burn in his throat. 'There's nothing to discuss.'

She flinched.

He closed his eyes. Shut out the image of her waiting for

him to expose his feelings. As if his hurts could fix hers. They couldn't. They hadn't helped his mother. Once, he'd felt. Once, he'd loved. Once, he'd offered his small arms to his mother. Tried to wrap them around her. Hold her. But it hadn't helped her. His feelings had drowned her.

'You said you needed closure with your dad,' she reminded him, 'but you didn't get it.'

His eyes snapped open. 'We are not,' he said and paced a step closer to the sofa, 'talking about my father.'

'I don't want to talk about him,' she admitted. 'I want to talk about our son. But I want you to understand why I'm asking to talk about Isaak now. I wanted closure too, with my dad,' she ploughed on. 'I thought when he died, when my mum died,' she continued, 'I would. But I didn't. Because I never talked about the things I needed to. I kept them all inside me. I never told my mum about my dad's affair. She died never knowing my father was a liar. That he spent days living another life, with another family.'

His gaze narrowed.

Her bottom lip trembled. 'His *other* family.'

'His other family?'

She nodded stiffly. 'I have brothers and a…a sister. She's the same age as me.'

'How did I not know you have brothers? *A sister?*'

'Because it's shameful.'

'Your dad was the cheat, not you.'

'But I knew. I knew where he was going, what he was doing, and I never told her.'

'You were protecting her,' Konstantinos supplied for her.

'No. I was protecting myself,' she confessed. 'My mum died never knowing I was a liar, too.' She shrugged a heavy shoulder. 'I lied,' she summarised heavily. 'All my life, my father lied. He used his love as a weapon. My father turned me into a liar by omission, because I wanted him to love *me*. So I kept his secrets from Mum to not shatter the family I wanted to have. My dad, at home, with *me*. So yes, I lied for him. For myself. And *I* hate what I did. I hate what I let myself become. I'll never be able to beg for my mother's forgiveness. I will never have closure.'

She was being painfully honest. *Too honest*. Never had they gone deeper than concise facts about their lives before they'd met. But never did Poppy lie. Unless under duress, he conceded.

Her dad had put her under pressure.

He himself had asked her to return to the spotlight, and she'd told him she wouldn't lie. Not even for him. Her husband. And he'd pushed her—made her agree.

He'd made her a liar, too.

Guilt snapped inside him like a tightly strung elastic band.

'It was your father,' he said, 'not you.'

'No.' Her blonde hair teased at her shoulders with the shake of her head. 'It was me,' she corrected, colour heightening her cheeks, hinting at the shame within her.

A shame he recognised. He'd tried to blame his father at first. Blame him for his mother's death. But he knew, too, it was him.

He didn't speak. *Couldn't*. Because how did he empathise without exposing his own wounds? His own weaknesses? He didn't want to be weak. Not in the eyes of the public. Not in hers.

'My relationship with my father, it was the reason I left without asking you for the truth about *that* photo. But the fact you didn't tell me about your father, by protecting me, you lied, too, Konstantinos. You didn't tell me where you were, or where you were going. You weren't open—*honest*. And that's why I left.'

'That's why you hated…*me*,' he finished for her, clarity forming in his mind.

He felt like a brute. *A bully*. So heavy-handed had he been with her. So hot had his rage run because of her abandonment. So high had the flames risen inside him when he'd found her and she'd spat her hate into his face.

He hadn't considered the reasons behind it. He'd only reacted. Let the anger guide him. And he had done it not to protect her, but to protect himself from *this*. Her pain. A childhood pain, he recognised, that spread its nastiness into adulthood, and shaped the people they'd become.

If you'd let her in, talked to her, you would have known these things about her. You could have helped each other.

He didn't know how to share his wounds. He didn't know how to help her with hers.

He stiffened. That was what therapists were for, and he'd employed one for Poppy.

'I hate liars, because *I* was the biggest liar, Konstantinos. My mum died never knowing the truth. If I'd confessed, if I'd talked to her, maybe I'd have closure. Maybe, if you'd talked to your dad, you would, too. Maybe, if we talk to each other about our issues, our parents, maybe we can talk about our son. Find closure on our marriage, and move on with our lives.'

'I do not need to have a deathbed confession, Poppy. I'm not dying,' he said, but inside he was.

Her confession, it killed something inside him. Stabbed a wound so deep, it pained him in a place he couldn't name. Some would probably call it his soul, but he knew he'd sold that the day he vowed to change. To let his DNA flourish and become his father. But he didn't feel it flourish inside him now. He didn't feel the heat of his rage. *His anger.* But nor did he feel weak. *Soft.*

It was an ache inside him. A need for something he didn't know how to ask for. *What* to ask for to make it stop.

'No,' she agreed. 'But we both will. *One day.* And if you don't agree to do this, to talk to me honestly about what happened with Isaak, it will never be over. We will never have closure. Isaak, he was the catalyst to all of this. We need to be open about that. *About him.* We need to—'

'No,' he said thickly. 'I won't pretend to meet you where I can't. I cannot talk about…'

He closed his eyes. The confession too close to his lips. Too close was he to telling her he couldn't say his name. Not out loud. He couldn't force it however hard he tried.

'We can't go on like this,' she said.

He opened his eyes and met the watery depths of hers.

'I can't bear to think when this is over, that if I see you, across the street, if we end up in the same room, we didn't do this properly. I want to do this—*end us*—with grace. With honesty.'

Konstantinos recognised it was a stand-off. A new kind of fight. And his wife would accept nothing other than his surrender.

He wouldn't wave a white flag. He couldn't give her what she wanted. But he'd give her a little of what she'd asked for. A little of the man he'd been. He'd be...*fair*. It would be an exchange. A story for a story. What would it hurt to do so?

'I will,' he said with a casual laziness he didn't feel, 'explain why I didn't tell you about my father.'

'You told me,' she reminded him. 'In Paris.'

'I didn't tell you everything.'

It was heavy in his chest.

This load he was trying to drag up from the depths he'd buried it in.

Her blue gaze narrowed. '*Everything?*'

'My mother died.'

'I know,' she said. 'When you were young.'

'She died because I couldn't keep her safe.' His throat threatened to close. He held it open. 'My mother died because *I* couldn't protect her.'

'I don't understand.'

'I couldn't risk it happening again,' he admitted, and closed the distance between them.

He didn't sit on the sofa opposite her. He sat beside her, and Konstantinos gave Poppy what he could.

'I could not risk it happening to *you*.'

CHAPTER TEN

It was a sledgehammer to Poppy's chest.

'You thought if you told me… *I'd die?*'

He looked at her for a tense, silent minute. 'What worried you about telling your mother the truth?'

'I wasn't worried the truth would *kill* her.'

'But you were,' he rejected. 'Not about causing her physical death,' he conceded. 'But the death of everything you were clinging to by not revealing your father's secret. You were scared, Poppy. Scared the truth would hurt all those you cared for.'

Her heart stuttered.

Was *he* scared?

'You *were* worried,' he continued. 'Worried if you revealed it, the world you were trying to hold together would crumble. So you held it together any way you could.'

The little girl inside Poppy who had wanted to tell her secret to someone, so she wouldn't be alone.

He understood why she'd done what she'd done. However selfish her choices had been, he didn't diminish the difficulty of those choices. But it didn't explain his.

'But you weren't close to your dad,' she countered. 'I certainly wasn't. His death, it would have changed…*nothing.*' She sucked in a loud, shuddering breath. 'I'm sorry, that sounds so horrible. He was your dad, but he wasn't. Not in any way that meant anything, Konstantinos. Not in a way that would have affected us.'

'I was worried, for you. So much death, Poppy. It had surrounded us. The threat of it. And then the reality of it,' he admitted, and his emotive honesty, it rounded her eyes. Lowered her jaw.

He *was* scared.

'I didn't have a close bond with…*him*, but you were sick—fragile. I wasn't prepared to risk another death—the proximity to it—would have broken you.'

'You think I'm breakable?' she whispered.

'Not when we met,' he replied. 'But you changed… *After…*' His neck corded. 'I saw your fragility then.'

'I was grieving.' A soundless sob clung to the inside of her throat. 'It would have changed you, too, if you'd accepted Isaak was part of our lives.'

'He wasn't. There was nothing to accept,' he said again as if it was a mantra. A coping mechanism to trick his brain to respond to the repeated statement. As if he was making himself believe it was true. As if Isaak's short time in their lives hadn't affected them.

It had.

Her chest burned. 'How can you be so…*cold*?'

His jaw ticked. 'He was gone, Poppy.'

Poppy stared at him. His eyes not vacant, but haunted. Was he haunted by their son, too? The what-ifs and maybes of what could have been? Secretly, beneath his public and personal persona, did he hurt too? Had *she* missed the signs? Her brow furrowed. There had been no signs. A shadowed look meant nothing. *Did it?*

'You just carried on as if life was normal. As if nothing had changed,' she said prompting him to change his mantra. Prompting him to be honest.

'Nothing *had* changed, but you refused to move on from

a situation that didn't exist any more,' he dismissed, as if her grief had been nothing. But it had been everything. Grief had riddled her bones, and yet he...

He was pure stone. Impenetrable. *Immovable.*

'How can you sit there talking about our son—Isaak—as if he didn't change everything? As if he didn't change us?'

His shoulders rose. Exposing the hard lines of him. His unbreakable body. Not an ounce of fat. Just muscle and sinew. Strong. *Powerful.*

She wasn't like him. Her body was soft, and she was all too aware of that softness now. The juxtaposition of her body—her internal self—compared to his.

'My mother's death broke me,' he confessed. 'Inside I was a mess. My father didn't let the mess spill out. He made me keep it hidden. My grief. He thought *that* would make me strong. And he was right. If I hadn't panicked when my mother walked into the sea—I could have saved her. If I didn't love her, I would not have gone into the water after her. If I had kept my emotions—*my feelings*—out of the situation I could have saved her. I had to be strong when he died. I am strong, Poppy, because I do not feel. I do not love. Because when life hurts—I know I can be strong for you. I was strong when Isaak died, because you couldn't be. Because *you* felt too much,' he said. 'I did my duty. I did it all because *you* couldn't,' he continued. 'You were just like my mother, and I... I needed to protect you as I hadn't protected *her.*'

Her eyes rounded. 'What?'

'My mother, she was always so sad. Sad about...*everything.* Her mental health...her mind...it was broken. She didn't function. She couldn't care for herself. She could not brush her hair. I brushed it. She would not eat. I fed her. And you...seeing you so broken, Poppy. I wouldn't let you disappear completely as she did.'

She shifted, brought her bottom to the edge of the cushion

and glared at him. 'I wasn't broken, Konstantinos. I was depressed. A medical condition I got help for. Help I no longer need.'

'But you did need it. *Help* I couldn't give you.'

'Yes,' she agreed. She wasn't ashamed of the deep depression she'd fallen into. 'But I also needed you to be there for *me*, and you put me in another bed—on the other side of the monastery. You left me alone, Konstantinos.'

His gaze flicked to hers and held. 'You pushed me away before the pregnancy was even deemed a risk.'

'We both struggled with the news of the pregnancy, Konstantinos,' she admitted. 'I'm aware of the gulf between us… It started then, but it came from you, too. You distanced yourself from *me*.'

And it had started the day she'd told him about Isaak.

Three times she'd taken the pregnancy test before she'd told him. She'd watched the pink lines appear, and turn from a faint pink to an almost vivid red. And those red lines had slashed through the foundations of their relationship. Torn them in two, until they had stood alone, so far apart from each other, and from what they had been.

Friends.

She'd started to prep for Isaak's arrival—rounding corners, placing guards in front of marble fireplaces.

He'd watched her planning and executing changes to the monastery with narrowed eyes.

He'd stopped coming to bed with her growing bump.

He'd stopped talking to her.

He'd stopped wanting *her*.

Their friendship had failed because it was only based on the good times. It wasn't a friendship at all if it couldn't hold up with the strain of reality, she realised.

'I was there for you,' he continued, 'in the only way I could be useful. Emotions…they only confuse things. Make people irrational. My mother… I didn't know it when I was a child. I thought it was just…*her*. But she was depressed. *Sick*. My presence didn't help her. She needed a doctor. She needed more than me.'

'That's how you knew *I* needed help?' she asked. She'd thought it was just grief that kept her in bed, or staring unseeing out of the window. It had been Konstantinos who had called the doctor.

'I recognised the signs.' His chest lifted with a sharp intake of breath. 'But I did not abandon you,' he rejected. 'I employed people. Everyone you needed. You were never alone. All the help you required was at your disposal.'

Her bottom lip trembled. 'I needed…*you*,' she confessed, because she had. Despite their rules. No emotions. No love…

'You didn't want me close. You wanted to focus on the baby. I provided everything for you to do it safely. And then when he was gone you were different, and I didn't know how to help you. Other than to be strong for you.'

'I couldn't tell you how I felt because you didn't want to hear it. You never did, and I didn't know how to tell you I was lonely. So lonely with you standing right beside me,' she admitted raggedly.

Konstantinos radiated tension. Every line of his body a tightly coiled spring.

'I wasn't what you needed to recover. I employed people,' he continued. 'People who could help bring you back. People who hadn't been called for my mother. *They* helped you.'

Was that what he'd been afraid of? Had he dealt with his grief through action? Had he buried his loss—*his pain*—trying to fix her? Had he been afraid that if he'd stopped, he'd crumble?

Action, planning for the birth of her son, it had given her strength. *Momentum*. Even on bedrest, the planning hadn't stopped. Her mind had been in action. But when Isaak died…

She'd crumbled.

'But when I found out about my father, it wasn't a decision I took lightly not to tell you.' His hands clamped together. 'But you could barely speak,' he continued thickly. 'You were barely alive… The past gives us choices, Poppy. We can use what happened to us before—*in the past*—to make different choices. But if we choose to do things differently, we must respond accordingly. We must demand different outcomes. And *I* demanded it would not be the same with you. It would be different.'

'*Different?*'

'My mother, she committed suicide.'

Her eyes blew wide. She knew that his mother had died. She knew it had just been his father, when Konstantinos was a teen, but she hadn't known *that*.

'I'm so sorry you had to go through that. Her…*suicide*.' She shook herself. Tried to clear her mind, focus in on what he was telling her and why. But she couldn't understand it. All these words he said that had nothing to do with *them*. 'But what does your mother's death have to do with you not telling me about your dying father?'

'It has everything to do with it. Just as you running from me—away from our marriage—had everything to do with yours.' He dipped a too tight shoulder. 'I was responsible for my mother. I knew she couldn't help it. It was *my* job to protect her. Even from herself.'

'That was your dad's job.'

'He wasn't there. *I was*. I watched my mother walk into the sea and I couldn't save her.'

His mother had abandoned him and so had his father. And she hurt for him. For the responsibility he'd been given when he was just a child to take care of his mum. But—

'I'm not your mother,' she whispered. 'I was never—*ever*,' she promised, 'going to do anything like *that*.'

'I don't know if my mother planned to do it either. There was no note. But the current. *The tide*. I wasn't strong enough to pull her body back to shore. I should have stopped her before she went into the sea. I should have saved her. But I didn't. I couldn't because emotion…' His lips curled into something ugly. 'I panicked, and she drowned.'

It hit her then. Hit her with the force of a bullet. She'd thought his distance was indifference. It wasn't. It was a coping mechanism. He kept his emotions inside. *Buried deep.* He didn't let them out. Any of them, because he needed to stay in control.

Her nose pinched.

He'd stayed in control when Isaak died because he had to.

It was the only way he could cope.

It wasn't a lack of feeling.

He felt. *Deeply.*

Her heart broke for him. For the little boy who believed his mother's death was his fault, and for the man who still thought the same. For the man who couldn't grieve openly for his son because…

Did he think it was his fault?

She knew it wasn't logical, but she'd blamed herself too. Still did, despite the therapy…

'I'm so sorry, Konstantinos.'

He stared at her. 'I vowed I would save *you*. It was my job to make sure I did not find you in the sea, held under by green weeds I could not cut you free from… I searched the world to find you… I prayed I was not too late, Poppy.'

He'd stopped his life. He'd stopped *everything* to find her. A man who did not let himself worry about anything, but he'd worried for *her*. He *had* saved her. He'd pulled her out of her deep depression. Provided the tools for her to crawl out.

Who had saved *him*?

Her mind reeled. Her emotions were being dragged in too many opposing directions. Her heart wanted it. More words. *More stories.* Words they should have said, stories they should have told each other long before they'd ended up here. But their self-imposed limits and rules had stifled the truth. They'd only really connected with raw honesty in bed. But without love, their marriage was hollow.

It always had been.

Superficial safety.

They'd never had strong enough foundations to survive Isaak's death.

'Whatever happens between us in these upcoming months,' he said, and she knew it was over. Whatever door he'd opened into himself, he was closing it.

She wanted to prise it back open.

'Know I am grateful, Poppy,' he told her. 'Grateful I found you.' His shoulders rose. 'I am grateful that you are...*okay.*'

He was...*grateful*?

Her heart ached behind her breastbone.

She'd let him down like everyone else.

'Now you understand why I didn't tell you,' he said. 'And my reasoning is as valid as yours. You ran because you believed, however brittle your proof, your life was taking the same path as your mother's. That I was an adulterer like your father. And you believed *that* because of your childhood. I believed I had to keep you safe from a truth that could hurt you because of mine.'

She stared at him. This man who had done everything to be better than the past that could have broken him. *Should* have snapped him in two. And to the world it hadn't. But she could see it now.

Inside, he was as broken as she was.

Her chest pitched tightly.

He wasn't ready to talk about Isaak, was he?

Would he ever be ready?

It had taken her time, too. Time to say his name without bursting into tears. Time to face her grief...

He sat so close to her. If she leaned in, shifted her bottom a few inches to the left, they would touch. Their knees. But the distance was a wall. A wall she'd put between them. They both had. She wanted to knock them down. Crawl into his lap and—

Poppy reached for him.

Konstantinos caught her wrist before her fingers touched him. Before she broke the divide between them. Cancelled out the distance. A space full of too many ghosts of the past *he'd* resurrected.

He knew his story was too dark. *Too ugly.* He never should have told her anything, he realised, but he didn't know how to take the words back.

He didn't want her pity.

He did not want her to touch him.

'What are you doing?' he asked, but it was too late. He'd breached the gap. *He* had touched her, and instead of putting her hand from him, he was holding it. Suspended in the air between them.

'*This.*' She pushed against the imprisonment of his fingers, and his wrist was weak. His hand fell.

She moved her hand to his shoulder. She clutched at the rigid arc. Her legs rose, and she used him to propel herself onto the sofa. Until she was on her knees—leaning in.

His nostrils flared. He breathed her in. *Too deep.* He could taste it. *Taste her.* The gentle husk of her sweet breath on his lips.

He closed his eyes.

Their mouths met.

His blood roared.

He didn't know how to tell himself not to do this. He didn't know how to tell his hands not to span her waist, to lift her until she was on his lap. And so he did not tell himself anything.

He couldn't think.

He didn't want to think any more.

His mouth pressed harder against hers. His tongue sought

entry into her mouth. Poppy opened for him. Let him inside. She didn't resist. She straddled him. Her bare thighs pressed to his. Her chest pushed against his, her pebbled nipples teasing him. Reminding him of the barrier of his shirt when all he wanted was to be in nothing but his skin.

'*Konstantinos!*' she gasped into his mouth. Her fingers spearing into his hair, cupping the back of his nape. She pulled him harder against her.

His hand splayed between her shoulder blades. He possessed her mouth. Owned it. He stroked—*he teased*—until he felt her hips press down. Until he felt her rock against his erection, pulsing against the confines of his too tight trousers.

He'd become so hard. So fast. And he ached to tear her T-shirt over her head, to feast on her pink nipples, drag her shorts down her hips. Free himself. Thrust up inside her. End this confessional in the only place he let himself lose control. *Inside her.*

'Stop,' he groaned, but still she kissed him. Still she rocked.

'I want you,' she breathed into his mouth, each word expelled on a pant. A hiss of air. A moan of desire.

It pummelled his brain. *This victory.* This was what he wanted. He wanted her to want him. He wanted her to need him. But he didn't feel powerful. He didn't feel in control. He felt raw. Exposed by the words he'd given her. *Told her.* Words he'd said to no one.

She shouldn't be on his lap.

She should not want him *now.*

'*Poppy!*' It was a cry of agony. It bellowed from his chest. '*Stop!*' His hands gripped her shoulders, dragged her mouth from his.

Both breathing hard, they stared at each other.

Regret tortured his insides. He felt haggard. *Old.* His bones ached with a fatigue he'd never known. It was rooted in his very skin. His muscles.

How could he have ever thought his plan was an option? His

plan, so flawed, it slapped his cheeks now. Slapped the controlled lines from his features he'd presented to Léon—*to her*.

Was he truly cruel? Ruthless? Like his father? Was he really going to let himself forget the people behind his needs? His father had forgotten his mother. Abandoned her. He'd forgotten *him*.

He couldn't continue.

Not with his plan.

Not with *this*.

He removed his hands from her shoulders, let them fall to his sides, and he demanded his fingers didn't curl into fists. 'We must stop.'

'Do you want to stop?' she asked. 'Or are you stopping because you think I'll regret it if we sleep together?'

'You *would* regret it.'

'At Versailles I would have,' she agreed. 'It would have happened with so much still misunderstood between us. But we've told each other things that will give us some emotional closure, but not physical closure.' She tilted her head—considered him for a beat too long. 'We should sleep together.'

'We should not,' he rejected, but he was torn. *Conflicted*. He didn't know how to put himself back together. Not with her eyes watching him so intently. Not with her sat on his lap—*wanting him*—when he'd told her of the ugliness inside him. The darkness of a sick mother and a power-crazed bastard of a father.

He was his parents' child.

He was damaged. He knew this. Had recognised it and so he'd made himself a man who rejected his very DNA.

He had never wanted children. Never wanted to risk passing on his genes to an innocent child. But they had made Isaak. And somehow, he'd manifested his son's death.

His chest tightened. He'd made himself a fair man. A man so opposite to his father. But beneath all the layers—beneath both the two personas he'd tried to be, he couldn't be either right now. He could not reconcile himself with them. They felt imaginary. *Fake.*

'I understand why you stopped at the ball,' she said when he didn't speak. *Couldn't.* 'But if we use a condom, there will be no risk.'

'There's *always* a risk, Poppy,' he countered, because it was the truth.

There were no one hundred per cent safeguards.

He couldn't promise that.

The only way to guard themselves completely against an accident was not to have sex.

His core spasmed.

But he wanted to.

He wanted her.

'We'll be careful,' she said, and he knew that was all they could be. *Careful.* But it didn't feel like enough.

The rules had changed when she'd become pregnant. Everything had changed. *Emotions*, hers, had leeched into their relationship. He wasn't stupid, he knew they'd leeched from him, too.

Poppy had carried his child. She'd swelled with their son. He'd have done anything to keep them safe. His need to do *that*…

It was a violent desperation. A desperation that had coordinated his every action. And when she'd disappeared… His desperation to find her, it had blinded him to all else, to the detriment of his business. His reputation.

He couldn't let emotions leech now.

He couldn't allow her in. *Close.* But he *was* desperate.

Desperate to be inside her.

'Why shouldn't we do this?' Her hand moved from his shoulder. Her fingers inching towards his face. Her thumb, so small, pressed to his bottom lip. Gently she dragged it across his skin. 'I won't regret it,' she said, her words uneven.

This didn't feel fake.

This chemistry between them. Heating her cheeks—controlling her words. Controlling the involuntary fall of his mouth.

This had never been fake.

'One last time,' she said, her eyes dipping to his mouth. 'For closure.'

'*Closure?*' he repeated.

'I regret many things, Konstantinos,' she admitted, and he now knew the truth of those words.

He understood the weight she carried on her too small shoulders of regrets that never should have been hers to have. Her father should have protected her. Whatever he did outside of their family home, it never should have been his daughter's secret to keep.

'I don't want to regret you,' she continued. 'I know now, however hard it was to tell each other our stories, it's not enough.' Her hand fell from his mouth. 'We need to do this. We need to wrap up…close the door—on everything. Including *this*.'

She moved. Only a fraction but every part of him hardened. Pulsed.

'*Hssss!*' His teeth gritted, he dug his fingers into her thighs and dragged her harder on the pulsing heat of him.

She gasped. 'Konstantinos…'

Closure. It was such a small word. It was such a necessity, he realised now. *For them both*. And the only place they would find it… His chest rumbled. It would not be on the sofa. He would not fuck her *here*. Like an out-of-control teen. Without a condom. Without the extra protection he could provide.

'We will sleep together,' he decided out loud, his hands moving to the bare flesh of her outer thighs. He smoothed his thumbs down the seam of them. Her spine curled with the downward stroke of his fingers.

'Yes,' she agreed.

It was a breath in his ear. A single word. But it felt like a storm. It attacked him from every direction. His mind. *His senses.* He couldn't pinpoint the attack. Where this single word hit him hardest.

'Make love to me,' she said, so forthright in her needs.

He ignored the drag in his gut. The ache in his chest. He felt all twisted. His thoughts. His insides… *He* didn't make sense. *This* didn't. It contradicted…*everything.*

'Not here,' he growled. It was raw. *Animalistic.*

'Then where?'

He'd take her to a place where they made sense. A place where they'd always found each other. Where words were never difficult.

He'd take them back to the place where they'd started.

He placed his hands on her hips, held her against him, and he stood.

It was fate for him to do this. For the war to end between them *there.* For them to lay down their arms and surrender to the inevitable in the place where they'd begun, and their marriage would end.

'We will go to bed.'

CHAPTER ELEVEN

Poppy buried her face in his throat.

He moved fluidly. One long stride after the other, as if her weight was nothing. As if his arms had been built to carry *her*. He'd picked her up many times, but this, it felt different.

It should feel as if they were saying goodbye, but somehow it felt as if they were saying hello.

Konstantinos's footsteps slowed. She raised her head. Opened her eyes. Light from up on high streamed down on his golden skin. Into his eyes. So dark. *So deep.*

Her head turned towards a door of tanned wood.

He reached for the handle.

Opened the door.

He stepped into the room of stark whites and velvet browns. Into the room made of windows and light. He hit a button and the caramel blinds closed out the view of the terrace, the pool, the sea and the cliff-top forests.

Until it was only them.

The orange light outside filtered through the seams of the blinds, softening the blanket of darkness. He hit another button. The bedside-table lamps lit up on either side of the bed.

A low bed. So wide. *So deep.* She knew she could get lost in its neutral-toned sheets. She knew the plump white pillows on the left and the right had separated them long before she'd moved to her own room.

There would be no divide now.

He carried her towards the bed. Laid her down in the centre. On his knees, he stood between her parted thighs.

'Kiss me,' she pleaded.

She wanted there to be no thoughts in her head.

She wanted only him.

He lowered himself. His mouth hovered in front of hers. Their breath mingled. Teased each other.

'Where do you want me to kiss you first?'

Her toes curled. 'On my mouth?'

'*Here?*' He pressed his mouth to the seam of her lips.

'Yes.'

He moved to the other side. 'And here?'

Butterflies took flight in her stomach, and their wings, so hard did they beat. 'Yes.'

He raised his head. 'And finally…' His eyelashes fell. Shadowed his high cheekbones. '*Here.*'

She held her breath.

Her eyes closed.

He pressed his mouth to hers.

It was an explosion. Too many wings took flight. Her mouth opened. His tongue crept inside. And all she felt was the need to be closer. To press herself against him.

Her fingers went beneath his suit jacket. Pushed it from his shoulders. His hands crept underneath her T-shirt. Their mouths parted as he yanked it over her head. And then his mouth was on her again.

Her fingers reached for his throat and yanked the knot of his tie free.

His fingers undid the button on her shorts, as hers found the buttons on his shirt, and freed them from their housing. She pulled his shirt free from the hem of his trousers.

He trembled. A full-body shudder. 'Poppy…' Panting hard, he pulled back. 'Lie down,' he commanded.

And she did.

He tugged her shorts down her hips. She curled for him, her knees, her ankles, until the shorts fell to the floor.

Mouth open, he stared down at her. His eyes moving over the rise and fall of her breasts inside her white bra. He tugged down the straps, the cups. His head dipped. He closed his mouth around her nipple. He sucked it.

'*Ahh!*' Poppy screamed.

She didn't notice his fingers going to her back. She didn't notice him unclip her bra until it was falling to the floor beside her. Until he was lifting his head.

He ran his fingers over her pelvis. Over the plane of her stomach. She watched his brown fingers tease at her pale flesh.

She'd always loved his hands. His fingers knew just where to touch her. He knew how to tease her, when to go slow. When to go fast.

She didn't need slow now.

'Konstantinos, please…'

He dipped his fingers inside the elastic band of her knickers. His fingers gently feathered over her blonde curls. He touched her intimate lips. Stroked her.

She trembled.

He dipped a finger inside her. A testing finger.

'Better?' he asked.

'That's good,' she husked, and pushed herself onto his hand, needing more, needing his fingers deeper. 'So good, but…'

He pushed another finger inside her.

Her eyes closed at the fullness. At the stretch of his fingers.

'Yes,' she moaned. '*More.*'

'Another?'

'*Please.*'

He pushed three fingers inside her. Gave her the fullness she needed. He curled them upwards. Found that secret nub of nerves deep inside her. Stroked it.

'*Ah!*'

She opened her eyes, raised herself on one elbow and reached for the open seam of his shirt, and yanked him closer.

His fingers still inside her, he came willingly. Met her where she waited for him. Crushed her mouth, dipped his tongue inside and filled it.

The pressure of his lips pushed her back into the pillows.

His fingers moved, almost pulling out.

He thrust back inside.

'*Konstantinos!*' She dipped her hands inside his shirt, pushed it over his shoulders. Dragged her nails over his taut flesh.

One arm freed, his shirt remained trapped on the hand bringing her to wanton extremes. Extremes making her skin burn. Her body restless to find release. It was so close. But it wasn't enough. She needed him naked. *Them naked.*

She dragged her mouth from his. He stared down at her. His fingers slowing. It was agonising. She wanted his hand back. But she knew it wouldn't be enough. She wanted his skin on hers. She wanted the weight of his body on hers.

'Take off your clothes,' she demanded heatedly.

His fingers slipped out of her. He raised himself again on his knees, and took off the shirt hanging on a single wrist. Threw it onto the ground beside the bed and reached for the buckle of his belt. The button.

She wanted to taste him.

She wanted what he'd denied her at the ball. To take charge. And this was the last chance she'd have to do it. She needed to do all the things she wanted to do to him. She needed to close the door on every fantasy. Leave no room for regrets.

She sat up. 'Let me.'

He hovered above her.

She unbuttoned him. Pushed her fingers into the band of his trousers, his boxers. She pushed them down his thighs. He sprang free. The sight of him, so hard, so thick…his erection stood proud between them. A wet heat flooded between her thighs.

She pushed his clothes down until they could go no further. Until they bunched around his knees. She flicked her tongue against the tip. Captured the droplet beading there.

'Poppy…'

She opened her mouth, leant forward and closed her lips around him.

His fingers drove into her hair. He didn't pull her closer, didn't angle his hips so her mouth took him further inside.

He waited for her.

She took him into her mouth. *Deeper.*

'*Theos mou!*' he moaned.

It was electrifying.

She moved her mouth up and down his silken length. He pulsed. Danced inside her mouth, until he grew bigger. *Thicker.*

Her hands reached for him, for his hips to lever herself. He moved with her mouth. Faster she took him. Faster he moved.

His hands cradled her scalp. His fingers tightened. '*Poppy!*'

He pulled her head back. Pulled himself free of her mouth. He stared down at her as if she was someone he didn't recognise. As if she made him burn. Made him lose his mind.

She didn't recognise herself—the smile tilting her lips.

It felt good for him to look at her like *that*.

'I will taste you,' he said, breathlessly. '*Now.*'

'I want you to,' she admitted, just as breathlessly. Just as awed by him. By what he'd just let her do when he'd never let her before. She'd tried once before to taste him, in the early days, but he'd stopped her. She'd shied away from trying again.

A niggle of doubt drooped her lips.

He hadn't let her make him come.

'Lie back against the pillows,' he said, kicking off the clothes bunched around his knees with a slide of his foot to the floor.

She dragged her bottom up. Lay down.

He moved up the bed between her thighs.

He dipped his head.

His tongue licked her inner thigh. He moved his mouth inwards. Pressed hard, deep kisses to the seam of her knickers. His tongue swept the place where he had kissed. Long, steady strokes. On the left. On the right.

Her fingers raked through his hair. She gripped the black silk. *Tightly*. Pulled it. She lifted her hips. She wanted his mouth there.

'Patience, *pouláki mou*.'

She wasn't patient.

The barrier of her knickers was too thick. Too unnecessary. 'Take them off,' she demanded.

He didn't lift his head. He didn't look at her. His eyes stayed focused on the part of her that needed more.

'*These?*' he asked, and his fingers ran down the seams, *slowly*.

Her toes pressed into the mattress. 'Yes.'

He gripped either side of her knickers. She lifted her bottom. Slowly, he pulled them over her hips. The fabric curled into itself as it travelled over her thighs, to her knees, her ankles and over the arch of her feet.

He dropped them to the floor with the rest of their discarded clothes.

His hands spanned her hips. Pushed them back into the mattress.

He kissed her. *There*. Teased at her with his tongue. Dipping it between her intimate folds. His mouth closed around her engorged nub.

'*Oh, my God!*'

He replied with his mouth. Sucked harder. *Faster*.

It wasn't enough.

'I want you inside me.'

'Not yet,' he whispered heatedly against the heart of her.

The warmth of his breath, of his mouth, the tease of his tongue dipping inside her—

It was torture.

'*Please*,' she begged, because it was the only word she had left.

She needed their last time to end with him inside her.

Konstantinos reached over to the gold handle of the bedside drawer. He opened it and withdrew a foil packet. He took out the condom and let the packaging fall to the floor.

His eyes met hers. His hand disappeared between their bodies. He sheathed himself, giving them an extra layer of protection.

The tip of him nudged at her opening.

'*Oh!*'

'Are you sure?' he asked, his voice a husk of broken need.

'I'm sure,' she replied just as brokenly. 'One last time.'

Konstantinos hesitated. He felt too big. *Too hard.*

'I don't want to hurt you,' he confessed raggedly.

'You won't.' She lifted her hips. Took him a little deeper.

His shoulders bunched. The knuckles of his hands bore down into the mattress.

'Poppy,' he growled, restraining himself, holding back months of denial.

He didn't want their last time to be quick. He wanted it to be slow. He wanted to taste every inch of her. But slowly—it was pain. It was agony.

The only way to make it end, he knew, was to push his hips forward. Bury himself deep, and pray he could remember his way out of the cocoon of her heat. That after, when it was over, he could forget how good she felt wrapped around him. *How right.*

This last time of theirs, it had to be enough.

It would be enough, he told himself.

Slowly, he pressed into her.

'*Konstantinos!*'

He buried himself inside her. Her intimate walls closed in. Enclosed him so tightly. He couldn't breathe for the pleasure of it. It was blinding. *Consuming.*

'Please… *Move.*'

He moved.

'Yes,' she moaned. '*Deeper.*'

He was lost. He arched his hips, buried his fingers into the bones of her hips and went deeper. So deep, he didn't know where he ended and she began.

He thrust again and again until she screamed his name.

'*Konstantinos!*' Her hips locked. So tightly did she squeeze him.

'*Poppy!*'

So hard did he come. It was bone-shattering. And he lost the will to hold himself above her. He collapsed on top of her. Buried his nose in her throat.

'That was…' she wrapped her arms around him. Panting just as hard as him '…*intense.*'

He made himself pull back—gather himself. His legs, his body screamed as he tried to move. But he did. He pulled himself free, rolled off her. He disposed of the condom in the bin beside the bed, ignored the stirring in his groin. So easy would it be to roll over to her, and do it again.

Konstantinos rolled onto his back. His brain rebelled. It told him to stand up and leave. Get out of the bed. To walk out the door and not look back.

Konstantinos did not get up.

He lay still. *Quiet.*

'Are you okay?' she asked, and rolled on her hip to face him. Her question, it made his eyes narrow. Had anyone ever asked him if he was…*okay*? He couldn't remember a time. And the question felt too blunt. Too visceral.

Her question, it probed him in tender places. *Vulnerable places*.

He wasn't ready to open those parts of himself.

He didn't know if he ever would be, or if he remembered how to access them.

'I'm okay,' she told him. She reached for him under the duvet. She placed the flat of her palm to his chest. To his heart thudding under the warmth of her delicate touch. It pounded as if it wanted out of his chest and into her hand. 'I'm more than okay, actually.'

'I'm fine,' he said, but it was ragged, each word a combination of exhaled breath and a touch of something that came up from the pit of his stomach. A something he couldn't name. But he didn't want it inside him.

Her hand stroked him.

Moved down to his stomach.

His sternum tensed.

She gasped. 'You're still hard.'

'It will go away.' He rolled onto his side, his face turned away from her, and shut off the light.

'Konstantinos—'

'Go to sleep, Poppy,' he said, and pulled the coverlet over his shoulders. His mind buzzed. With too many thoughts. Too many incoherent things. They were only flashes. Flashes of the sea. Of weeds. *Of Isaak*.

His son's face bloomed to life in his mind. His scalp a mass of straight black hair. Hair he'd raised to his nose. *Inhaled*.

Emotion too thick—*too fast*—clogged his throat. He fought the urge to reach for her. Wrap his arms around her small frame.

He would control his fingers. He would not reach for her

hip—drag her closer—into him. He would not bury his nose into her hair. *Inhale her.* He would not hold her.

He closed his eyes, and Konstantinos prayed that, whatever this was…this need to have her close…

It would go away.

CHAPTER TWELVE

A COLD QUIET slipped inside the bed with Poppy.

It settled over the room, over her skin, and whispered into her ears.

She didn't have to open her eyes. *She knew.*

Konstantinos was gone.

She rolled onto her stomach, pushed her face into the pillow. It hit her. His scent. *Theirs.*

The scent of heated desire long spent. Was it done? Did it feel like…*closure*?

It stirred in her stomach. *Arousal.* It narrowed to the sensitive place between her thighs. *Tender.* She felt him there. She felt him on her skin. Moving inside her.

She sat bolt upright—clutching the duvet to her chest.

The blinds were open. Only a little. Only enough to reveal the doors leading outside to the veranda. Her gaze swept over the room. It was chaos. Clothes—*evidence*—of what had happened yesterday was everywhere.

There hadn't been evidence in this room for longer than she could remember. It had become *his* room. Slowly, all of her things had left with her to the other side of the monastery. But she was here now. Her things were in his room. *She* was still in *his* bed.

She should have gone back to her room. She should have treated this as what it was. A one-time thing. A last time. Because being here now…

It didn't feel over.

It didn't feel like closure.

She was still naked. *Still aching.*

She needed to leave.

Go back to her room.

Poppy threw the cover off and pushed herself to the end of the bed. She dropped to the floor, on her knees, and doubled over reaching for her bra…

'Good morning, *glikia mou*.'

Her head snapped up. Her tangled hair heavy and knotted, it moved awkwardly on her scalp.

'Konstantinos,' she said, but it wasn't a greeting. It was an acknowledgement to herself. He hadn't left her. He'd been…

Her eyes flicked over his wet black hair, the droplets of water kissing his skin. A few stray drops ran down his broad shoulders, his curled bicep. Over his washboard-flat abdominal muscles. Her gaze flicked to the white towel in his hand.

'You've been swimming?' she asked, but she knew. It was an obvious statement. But she'd never understood it before. His routine to start his day doing endless laps. It hadn't occurred to her this morning he'd be doing it. It hadn't occurred to her why he did it.

It did now.

It thumped her on the temples.

It wasn't a fitness ritual.

It was to perfect his swimming technique.

It was to make sure he could fight against the tide.

'Why are you on the floor?' he asked.

She looked down at the bra in her hands. *Her nakedness.* On her knees, she moved closer to the bed. She didn't know why she felt the need to hide. Why she felt guilty. She held up her bra. 'Getting dressed.'

'Were you going to leave without saying goodbye?'

She understood it now. The darkening of his gaze. Its narrowed intensity as he awaited her reply. She was going to sneak out as though last night had been nothing but a one-night stand. Something casual. Something easily forgettable. But wasn't that what it was? What they'd agreed it would be? Something to be done and now they'd done it. Now they both had to forget it. Move on. Close the door.

'I thought you'd left already,' she admitted.

'I'm still here.'

Her breath caught. He was. And so was she.

The silence thickened until it pulsed with a low drumbeat of awareness. An awareness of the room where they stood. *The bed.* Of her nakedness. His near-nakedness. All he had on was black swim shorts. Wet, and clinging to his muscular thighs.

Her body forgot the rules. It tingled. Her feet ached to find the floor, to stand from her knees, and go to him.

She'd make herself remember what they'd promised to each other. She ducked her head. Hid her eyes from his, because she could feel the little blaze in them dilating her pupils. Her eyes found her shorts. She reached for them.

She looked up at him from behind lowered lashes. 'I'll get dressed,' she said.

He ran the towel over his head. 'I'm going in the shower.' He turned to his right and without looking at her again he opened the door, walked through it and closed it behind him.

The water started to run.

The memory hit her now.

The day she'd hired the private investigator; she'd stood outside this bathroom, listening to him run the water, knowing he was beneath it, scrubbing himself clean.

Her heart squeezed into a tight fist.

She'd been so very angry that day. It had swallowed her grief. Eaten her from the inside out. And when he'd emerged from the bathroom barefoot and shirtless, his trousers unbuckled, smelling of soap…

She hadn't been honest with him *that* day. And if she had been…

She wouldn't think of it. The past, it was just that. *Gone*. After everything they'd been through, didn't she owe him honesty now? Didn't she owe it to herself?

She'd been wrong.

Last night it hadn't been enough.

She stood, leaving her bra and shorts on the floor.

Naked, she walked to the bathroom.

Poppy placed her hand to the closed bathroom door.

A jittery flutter danced in her stomach.

It wasn't her nakedness that made her hesitate. It wasn't her bare flesh that made her feel vulnerable. If she opened the door—if she stood before him in nothing but her skin—and told him her truth, what she needed from him…*more*…would he reject her? Or would he listen?

She didn't have a solution. She just knew it hadn't worked. *This* wasn't closure. And she knew it was the same for him. Knew he stood in there now, thinking of her out here, while she thought of him in there…

What did she have to lose?

Poppy opened the door.

The bathroom was a wet room made of speckled white marble. It was huge. Gold-accented mirrors lined the walls. A claw-footed bath stood to her right, a his-and-hers sink to her left and in front of her…

Konstantinos stood beneath the shower head. His hands braced on the wall in front of him. His head ducked. The water beating down on his head. The water streamed between his shoulder blades, over the curve of his spine, to cascade over his firm buttocks.

Low embers of heat ignited in her stomach.

She swallowed, moved inside the room. The marble damp beneath her feet, she walked towards him.

Her heart racing, she stood behind him.

'Konstantinos.'

He turned, sweeping the hair away from his face. He dragged his fingers through it—combed it backwards. His black eyes met hers. Framed by thicker lashes now, darker.

He stepped forward, out of the stream of the overhead spray. Water dipped from every part of him. Down the tip of his noble nose. Rolled down his chest, flattening the wisps of his hair to his tanned skin. And lower. Arrowing down the V on his stomach.

The air stuttering from her lips, Poppy snapped her gaze back to his.

'I was wrong,' she admitted too quickly. *Too breathlessly.* 'Last night. It was…*intense*. It was good. But I… It wasn't enough, Konstantinos, and I don't know how to fix it.'

So intensely did he watch her. He didn't speak. Did not push her to say it quickly. He just waited for her to tell him what she wanted. What she needed. The feelings were there. In her chest. *Lower.* But the words…oh, how hard it was to think them, let alone say them. To admit she needed what she needed.

She needed him. *Still.*

'I want…' Her chest was on fire. Her shoulders rose with the breath she held inside her lungs for too long. She made herself exhale. She let the burn travel up her throat, until it was in her mouth, and she let them out. Her feelings. *Her truth.*

'I want more.'

So did Konstantinos.

All night he'd lain beside her. Wanting to touch. Wanting *her.*

He hadn't been able to admit having her back in his bed felt so right, but everything else… It was wrong. Inside, everything felt mismatched. Out of sync.

He'd thought the water, his disciplined stroke, would align him. But even in the water his body had been too stiff to pull him forward. He was sluggish. *Weak*. And finding her ready to leave when he'd returned…

His throat closed. He couldn't explain it. Why he hadn't been able to reconcile himself with the fact it was over. She was going back to her side of the monastery. They would continue their ruse, but everything else they'd promised to close the door on.

He didn't want to close the door. *Not yet*.

He ached to take control. To do what his body demanded he do, and take charge. Pull her beneath the water with him and kiss her. Push all this—whatever it was…it was a ball, a knot, a mass of something he couldn't expel, untie, or release—into her.

'What do you want to do, Poppy?'

'I want to come in,' she said.

'There are no shower doors,' he reminded her. 'There is nothing to stop you joining me in here.' But there was, he knew. It was why he hadn't reached for her last night. It was why he didn't reach for her now.

'We said one last time,' she said out loud for them both.

'It wasn't enough,' he said. 'For either of us.'

'No.' Heat flooded her freckled cheeks. 'It wasn't.'

'So we should do it again,' he said, guiding them both to the conclusion they both wanted. Both needed.

Her eyes blew wide. 'One more time?'

'As many times as it takes,' he countered. 'Until we reach the closure we desire.'

Her pert breasts lifted with a deep inhale.

He hadn't let himself see her nakedness.

He hadn't considered his.

He was aware of both now.

'Okay.' She exhaled it, her agreement, but there was more.

He wouldn't question it. He wouldn't analyse it. It was a requirement. A necessity. He would demand it, and she would give it to him. She'd give it to him because after last night, he saw it in her eyes.

There was no alternative.

'We will have your things moved back into the main suite,' he said, watching her watching him.

'We will,' she agreed.

'You will sleep in my bed,' he said, his voice rough. 'You will sleep with me every night until…' His voice simply stopped.

'Until after we renew our vows,' she supplied for him.

Stiffly, he nodded.

'I'll sleep with you every night, until then,' she confirmed, and that ache inside him… *That* thing he didn't know to ask for, because he didn't recognise it, what he needed to soothe it…

It shifted inside him.

'You will kiss me,' he breathed.

'I will,' she said and stepped closer to him.

Her toes, so small, so dainty, moved in front of his. His heart thudded as her long, slender fingers reached up to cradle his cheeks.

Then she was on the tips of her toes and her mouth found his.

Konstantinos closed his eyes. He couldn't move. He stood rooted. The pressure of her mouth, it was so soft. So gentle. Her lips lingered on top of his. Feathering over the seal of his. As if she were learning the shape of his mouth. As if this was new. A first kiss.

His hands went to her hips. He cradled them in his palms. Drew her in closer. The tips of her breasts met his chest.

He moaned. A guttural thing, it escaped his lips. Her mouth opened. She breathed it in. Breathed *him* in. As if he was supposed to be in there. A part of her.

His brain was addled. Fuddled by too many hormones, he told himself, and pushed his tongue into her mouth. *Deeply.*

'Konstantinos,' she breathed into his mouth, and whatever sense—whatever rationality that remained—disappeared.

He picked her up and she wrapped her legs around him. He

turned them both around, dipped them beneath the warm water and found the wall beyond it. He held her there.

He dragged his mouth from hers. 'I can't wait,' he admitted, because he couldn't not admit it. 'I need to be inside you, Poppy. So badly.'

He didn't recognise it. His voice. The desperate edge to it. It was gritty. It wasn't the voice of a man in control. It was the voice of a man who didn't know what control meant. As if he hadn't spent his life living by its definition.

'I need that, too,' she said, and kissed the edge of his lip, and then the other. 'I need *you*.'

He raised her bottom. The hard length of him arrowed to where it longed to be. Sheathed inside her. He dipped his hips forward and up.

Konstantinos thrust.

'*Yes!*' Her nails tore through his back. '*More!* Please, Konstantinos. *More*.'

Mindlessly, he thrust inside her. Again, and again. Chasing oblivion with her locked around his hips. Needing to find it.

'I'm going to come,' she half-screamed, half-sobbed. She sank her teeth into his shoulder.

He needed to slow down. He needed—

'*Oh, Konstantinos!*' Her intimate muscles clamped around him. Urged him to find his orgasm with her. And so desperately did he want to. So desperately did he want to come inside his wife. *Inside her*.

A war raged inside him.

He couldn't do it. He would not allow himself to lose himself so completely. To put her at risk. Instead he held her still, waited for the tremors to slow, for her breathing to return to some semblance of normal. Only then did he lift her. Break the intimate seal of their bodies.

'Konstantinos—'

'It is wet,' he told her. 'Mind your footing.'

He steadied her on her feet.

She looked down at his still hard, still straining erection, glistening with the evidence of their shared desire.

'You didn't come,' she said.

'The condoms are in the bedroom. We will go to bed,' he said, 'and I will make you come again,' he promised thickly.

'No,' she said, and she took him in hand. *Stroked him.*

He hardened. He was so hard he did not know it was possible for him to be so hard. So big was he, she could barely enclose her palm around him.

'I want to make *you* come,' she admitted. 'I want to kiss you. *Here.*'

Konstantinos stiffened. She'd offered him her mouth twice. And twice he'd denied her. He knew now, this wasn't a game of power, or of control. But still, he hesitated. Still, he remembered how it had made him feel before. *Vulnerable.*

Why should he not allow her to taste him?

Soon she'd be gone. Soon he'd let her go. Why shouldn't he allow himself *this*?

It would be a newness.

Not surrender.

'Yes, please, Poppy,' he said.

She fell to her knees, and took him into her mouth.

He braced himself on the wall above her with two hands.

The water hit his back, shielding her from the spray.

It was pleasure. It was pain. It was…*everything*. The tightness of her mouth. The flick of her tongue.

It was a gift.

Konstantinos watched her caress him. She braced herself on his thighs. He planted his feet as her head bobbed, and he prayed his knees wouldn't buckle as her caress deepened. So deep did it become, it had no end.

He closed his eyes. So intense was it, the sensation building inside him. He had no choice but to try and control it. But he couldn't.

It tore through him like a firework.

'Poppy!'

She didn't release him. She closed her mouth tighter around him as he spasmed inside the warm embrace of her mouth. Until it was over. Until the aftermath washed over him. Until the pulse of him was softer between her lips.

She released him from her mouth.

He looked down.

She looked up.

'Thank you,' he husked, and reached down for her. Helped her to her feet.

He shut off the shower.

'You're most welcome,' she said, almost shyly. As if she felt it too. The firsts. *The newness.*

He scooped her up in his arms.

She laughed. 'It's too wet for you to carry me!'

Konstantinos didn't laugh. He stared at her mouth. The sound it had made. Her laugh. So long had it been since he'd heard it. And *this* laugh… He wasn't sure he'd heard it before.

He wanted to hear it again.

His heart hiccuped.

He was a fool.

He moved back towards the bedroom.

'Where are we going?'

'Back to bed,' he said, and that was where he'd keep her. Where they would stay, until they could no longer stand the sight of it. Until they'd drained any newness from each other.

Until it was time to say goodbye.

Forever.

CHAPTER THIRTEEN

Two Weeks Later...

KONSTANTINOS COULDN'T FIND HER.

Every day, for the last two weeks, she'd been in reach of his mouth. His fingers. They'd started and ended each day *touching*. In bed. And the times in between...

He hadn't gone to work. He'd been here. *With her.* Inside her most of the time. His only goal to drive out their chemistry. Make the feel of her body on his, his body's response to her, something repetitive. Something he did by rote. Gave pleasure and took his in return. But still, it was not rote. It was not repetitive. *Sex.* With her...

It was never enough.

It never had been.

He wouldn't think of it.

It only lingered now, this fierce chemistry between them, because it had been so long since they'd been together.

It would go away.

It had to.

His hands curled into fists.

It flashed in his mind. Kyparissos. Tall evergreen trees named for the grieving. For those who mourned beneath them.

He knew where she was.

The *koimeterion.*

The sleeping place.

He followed the white stone walls, walked beneath the arched, too low ceilings where no windows let in the sun. It was a stone tunnel, built by the monks to lead them from community prayer to find their own sacred solitude. To take them out of the darkness into the light outside.

Reaching the end of the tunnel, Konstantinos opened the arched door, stepped outside. And up he went. Up the dusty stone steps warmed by a high sun. Down the path he'd enlarged to accommodate the procession.

Konstantinos had led them all carrying the white box with tiny gold handles on his shoulders to the too small piece of land that would forever be his son's home. A place where he would forever sleep. But he'd never been awake. Never alive. Never… *real*. Not in the way he was to Poppy. As if the time he'd spent inside her womb she had got to know him. *Love him.*

They came into view. The cypress trees at the top of the hill blocking out the sun and standing guard of those buried below their textured trunks. He hadn't wanted to bury him with his parents. Poppy hadn't wanted to bury him with hers. There had only been one choice. *Here.* On the island. In a graveyard exclusively for the monks. To bury him with other souls truly at rest.

His gut spasmed.

Had Isaak had a soul?

He reached the flat summit of the small hill.

His footsteps slowed. So quietly did she stand there, with her back to him, the only movement her white dress. The cotton pushing close against her skin. The wind blowing in from behind her. Her blonde hair was loose. It fell about her shoulders, moved in time with the rustle of the wind in the trees surrounding her.

A husk of softly spoken French teased at his eardrums. Swept to his ears by the grace of the breeze rustling the trees.

He frowned.

Was she singing? Singing to… *Isaak?*

Something sharp jabbed into his heart.

Their son could not hear her.

He crossed the distance between them, because his body would do nothing else. His feet dragged him closer. And he did not think. He did not question his need to do it. To be with her here in a place he hadn't visited. Did not want to visit. And yet, he was here. *With her.*

He stood beside her but found his eyes did not try to find hers.

They looked only at the grave now marked with stone, with *his* name.

Isaak Ariti.

It slammed into his chest. He felt the bones in his chest give way. *Crack.* Inwards. And they trapped the air he needed to expel inside his lungs. Until it burnt. Until it…*hurt.*

The pain, it wasn't imaginary. It was real. As real as the grave in front him. As real as…

Tentacles choked him from the inside. Wrapped around his throat and squeezed.

Or was that…?

He looked down. Her hand, it was holding his. Her fingers had slipped between his, entwined themselves around his. And she was…*squeezing.*

He raised his head. Looked into her blue eyes. She looked… *thoughtful.*

'We need to talk,' she said softly.

'Why?'

'The last two weeks… They've been good. So very good. But there is so much we haven't spoken about. Things *I* need to talk about, because it feels so heavy not to. I know last time was…*hard.*'

'Poppy,' he warned. He didn't need to do this. *Not here.* When the memory was all too real. An imprinted image in his head of her falling to her knees, carrying her to bed, and leaving her to sleep.

'I didn't get a chance to apologise to my mum.' She looked down at the hand she held. She placed her other on his. Trapped his between her much smaller ones. 'I want to apologise to you, Konstantinos.' She raised her head. '*I* was in the wrong, too, in our marriage. I see that now…'

Shame gripped him. She wanted to apologise to soothe her own guilt by owning her part in her pain. She needed to own it. He could see that now. And he recognised it. The need for it.

She needed to say sorry to him, because she'd never had a chance to say her sorries to her mother. Just as *he* hadn't. How could he deny her that? But he struggled to open his ears and accept it.

He'd made so many mistakes. With his mother. *With her.* He should have held her. He should have done so many things differently. He should have been by her side; however hard it was to see her like *that*. However it made him…*feel.*

It had been inhumane to close her off. But he didn't know how to apologise for his actions. He didn't know if it happened again, would *he* be different?

It wouldn't happen again.

'It doesn't matter,' he dismissed.

'But it does matter.' She snatched in a too shallow gulp of air. 'I'm sorry I didn't notice what you were going through with your dad. I'm sorry I was so wrapped up in myself I didn't see the little things, Konstantinos. I was your wife, and I didn't know— I didn't see what you were going through. I didn't consider it.'

'I do not need your apology. Not about…*him*. He will cause no more distress for anyone.'

'I'm sorry I wasn't there for *you*.'

'I didn't need you to be there.'

She ignored him. 'I'm sorry I didn't give you a chance to explain before I left.'

'You have explained now,' he said roughly.

'I was selfish.' Her neck, those delicate tendons inside her pale flesh, tightened. 'I'm sorry. For everything. I'm so sorry I pushed you away when I was pregnant.'

'Your mental health…' he offered up to her, as an easy end to this conversation. A ready-made excuse.

'It started before the pregnancy was even deemed high-risk. I can see that now. So clearly.'

'You were…' he thought of her exercise regime in the beginning. Her healthy eating. Preparing the nursery '…*nesting*,' he finished because that was how she'd appeared to him. Stockpiling her little twigs. Making her nest all alone. Without him. The nest had not been big enough for him to join them. She'd pushed him away. Disconnected from him, even then. Before he was…*gone*.

'I was hyper-focusing,' she countered. '*Obsessed*, with doing everything right.' Her gaze left his and flitted to the little grave in front of her.

He didn't turn. He kept his eyes on her. On the real woman in front of him. *Alive*.

He couldn't save Isaak, any more than he could have saved his mother.

'Your explanation about your…*family*. It helped me understand. It helped me understand…*you*. I'd like you to understand… *me*. A little more. I want you to know why I behaved like *that* when I was pregnant.'

'I already understand it,' he said. 'You were never put first as a child. So you put the baby first without hesitation.'

'I did,' she agreed. 'I put my needs before our marriage. Before…*you*. I did what had been done to me for my entire childhood by my father. What had been done to you for the entirety of yours. I put *you* second.'

'I'm not unaccustomed to the position,' he admitted because

too closely did she stroke *that* hurt inside him. An old pain now. But still it ached. Deep in his bones.

'It shouldn't have been that way for us.'

'But it was,' he reminded her. 'It was the only way *we* could be. The only way *I* could be.'

He needed his hand back. He needed to step back. Because oh, so close was she to knowing. Understanding all those things he'd never explained to anyone. Why he worked so hard to be number one. Why he was never second place in anything he did.

'Is that why you never wanted children?' she asked, digging, probing into parts of himself he didn't want to go. 'Because you never wanted them to come second best to business?'

'*Exactly*,' he answered truthfully. What was the point in denying it when she already knew? But still she pressed.

'That's why you hated him? The real reason you never took over your father's company? Why you made a rival business—became number one in the industry? You did it to be number one?'

'I did it for *her*.' His lips curled into something ugly. 'I did it to prove it didn't have to be like it was for my mother. No one had to be second best to business. *No one*. Not employees. Staff. Everyone could be treated fairly. *Equally*. No one had to be left behind. No one had to be alone. Like she was. My father left her to suffer. He locked her away from the public. He left me to look after her, and I…couldn't.'

He was breathless. His heart pumped as if he'd been in a ring with a boxer. Never had he confessed it. Never had he let anyone see why he had to be the man he was. Number one. Kind. Fair. *Loyal*. But he had told her.

'I'm so sorry I left you behind, too,' she said, and her apology stroked something inside him. Lifted it.

No one had apologised for leaving him behind. But she was. She was doing this because she thought he needed it. He couldn't let himself need it. Words, they meant nothing.

She was still leaving him. A few more months, and it would be over between them as if it had never happened.

A mist sheened her eyes. 'Oh, Konstantinos.'

His throat tightened.

He'd seen Poppy cry before. He understood why humans cried. It was a release of emotion from the only part of the body it could escape from. But for her to do it here. For her to cry in the place where the tears—*the emotions*—had buckled her knees.

He was scared, he admitted to himself, that this time he was too weak to carry her. His body didn't feel like itself.

He didn't feel strong in this place.

He felt…*undone*.

'We need to leave, Poppy,' he said. 'We'll go inside.'

'I don't want to go inside.'

'You are crying.'

'I am,' she admitted.

Something shifted inside him. And he didn't like it. He did not like the instinct raising his hand to her cheek. Or the words ready to spill from his mouth. But he did it anyway. He raised his hand, and the tremor beneath his skin, he couldn't hide it. He brushed his hand against her cheek—tried to wipe away the wetness, but another drop fell.

'Don't cry, *glikia mou*.'

'But I want to.'

'*Why?*'

'I miss him,' she admitted, so openly, so honestly.

'The baby?'

'Of course.' A trembling smile, so small, teased at her lips. 'I'm crying for all of us,' she admitted. 'For Isaak. For myself. I'm crying for *you*.'

No one had wept for him. Not his mother. Not his father. He hadn't wept for himself. *Ever*.

He didn't want her pity. He wanted to reject them—give

these tears back. This softness. This intimate empathy he didn't deserve.

'Do you want to go to bed?' The question was out of his mouth before he could stop it.

Her face twisted into a repulsed line of rejection. 'I don't want to have sex.'

'Do you want to *sleep*?' he corrected, remembering her all too many naps when the sadness had become too much. *Too unbearable.*

And this…it was unbearable to *him*.

'What will *you* do while *I* sleep?' she asked, her voice still uneven, *rough*, from too much spent energy.

'I'll be quiet,' he assured her. He didn't wish for quiet solitude. He felt *nothing*. Not pain. Not hurt. He didn't need to be soothed. But he longed to give her something.

Some kind of…*peace*.

'I will hold you.'

'No,' she rejected it. *Instantly*. Rejected him. His hold.

It was a kick to his knees. His mother had rejected him. His little arms. His weak arms.

'I will hold *you*,' she said.

He, of course, knew what it meant to be held. Open arms were offered to children when they cried. It was offered to everyone who demanded reassurance—*closeness*. Intimacy of a softer nature. It had never been offered to him. He didn't need that kind of softness. He'd never been offered it as a child and he didn't need it now he was grown.

He didn't need *this*.

He closed his eyes, but he couldn't stop his arms. He didn't want to. He wrapped them around her small frame. He couldn't control his fingers. He knew they pressed too hard into her hips. But he couldn't tell himself to be gentler. He pulled her in close. *Inhaled her.*

'Poppy,' he breathed into her hair.

A sound broke the hum of her shallow, quick breathing. A small sound. But it was primitive. Muffled. A sound of anguish. *Distress.*

Konstantinos recoiled.

The sound had come from *him*.

Poppy heard it.

Almost childlike. It was a tiny moan. A croak.

Her fingers flexed on his back, smoothed over the tension holding him too straight. *Too tall.* She could feel it in his body. The tension. The rejection of it. The sound that wanted to escape. *Be released.*

The fire returned to her nose—demanding she cry harder.

And oh, she wanted to.

She wanted to weep the tears Konstantinos could not. Had never allowed himself to weep. She wanted to wail for the little boy who'd lost his mother. She wanted to weep for the little boy who blamed himself for her death. She wanted to weep for the boy whose needs were neglected. She wanted to weep for the boy who no one had held.

Not even his wife.

Until it was too late.

Her fingers dug into his shirt. She scrunched it tightly in her fingers, afraid that if she didn't she'd crush him now. Hold him too tightly.

A sob bubbled in her chest. She caught it before it escaped. But a lump formed so large in her throat she couldn't swallow it.

She closed her eyes. So tightly they hurt.

She stopped crying.

Her tears wouldn't help *him*. But how could she help him? How did she teach him it was okay to feel when no one had shown him how? How did she show a man made of steel it was okay to bend? That she wouldn't let him break?

She kept her head pressed to his chest. Listened to the loud beat of his heart in her ear.

She couldn't. She knew this now. She couldn't teach him how to feel. She couldn't teach him how to accept the overload of what she knew now was inside him. But she could do *this*.

She could hold him.

She could be here for him.

They could be there for each other.

She raised her head from his chest, but she didn't release him. She kept him close. She understood what they needed now.

'Were you happy?' she asked.

His brows knitted. *'With what?'*

'The life you'd built for yourself? Were you happy with our marriage?' she clarified. 'Before—' she raised her right hand and gesticulated in a three-sixty turn '—were you happy with *me*?'

'Were you?' He flipped the question. *'Happy?'*

Isaak, he'd changed everything. But he never should have pushed them apart. He should have brought them closer together. She would let her son do that for them now. She would make it what it should have been. *Now.*

She stepped closer to him. 'I think we can be *happier.*'

'What do you mean?'

'I understand your choices so much better now,' she said. 'I understand—I know you—better than I did in our marriage. I understand myself better, too.'

And she did. She hadn't been wrong all those years ago to choose him. It had taken their separation, the reunion, the battle of marriage contracts and terms of divorce to see it.

But she saw it now. There was no one else for her. And there was no one else for him.

'All those choices I made before,' she started, and a single tear slipped free.

It hurt her now. The truth. Their marriage…they'd never really let it begin.

If only they'd realised sooner the battles they were fighting on their own to maintain those too high walls, they could have fought them together.

She wiped the wetness from her cheeks. Demanded they stop. 'I can't undo them,' she admitted. *Owned it.* Her mistakes. 'But I can make different choices now because of them. I can choose to fight. And *I* want to fight,' she admitted.

Puzzlement flashed in his black eyes. 'What do you want to fight about?'

'I want to fight for *us.*'

She released him. Let go of him and took a step back, because he needed to decide this was what he wanted too.

She'd thought she needed closure. In a sense, their conversations had given her *that*. But it had given her something else too.

It had opened a door, and she had a choice if she wanted to walk through it. If she wanted to claim the marriage they had wanted all those years ago. But this time it would be stronger, she knew this. Because *she* was stronger. She was different. *Changed.*

It would be different this time.

'I want to try again,' she admitted. 'I want to be your wife. *Forever.*'

A pulse flicked in his cheek. 'Forever is a long time, Poppy.'

'It's what I'm willing to commit to.'

'Why the change of heart?'

'Isaak never should have pushed us apart. He should have brought us together. Let our son do *that* for us now.'

The hard lines of him dipped with the slow expulsion of air. 'So much has happened, Poppy.'

'It has.'

'Do we still want the same things? A marriage based on loyalty, respect, without the complications of love?'

Love had always been such a dirty word.

It didn't feel that way now.

It didn't feel dirty when he spoke it.

It felt…*right*.

It was too late.

She'd fallen for him long ago, hadn't she?

She'd run away not because of her father, but because Konstantinos had broken her heart by pushing her away. Her fury—*her rage*—it had all come from a place of love.

She loved him.

She could see that now. *Feel it.*

He couldn't feel it, could he? This love?

He wasn't in the same place she was.

He wasn't ready to talk about Isaak.

He wasn't ready to…*feel.*

Maybe if she gave him time…

He stepped closer. 'Do you want a fresh start with the same rules?' he asked, his voice urgent, as if her silence made him anxious.

She nodded.

That would be enough, she told herself. *For now.*

CHAPTER FOURTEEN

Two Months Later...

Poppy walked down the aisle.

Sunlight streamed onto the path before her through the stained-glass windows, throwing rainbow colours onto every empty seat.

In three days, they wouldn't be empty.

The chapel would be full.

All eyes would be on them.

It didn't feel abstract any more.

She couldn't distance herself from it.

She could no longer trick her mind it was only a job. *An event.*

It was different.

She was different.

This time she wouldn't walk up the aisle to meet Konstantinos, knowing it was a marriage of convenience. She didn't carry the heavy burden of the walls guarding her heart.

Her heart drummed with her every step towards the arch made of wild flowers. The arch where they would meet at the altar.

The arch *she'd* designed.

In every corner of the chapel, this time, she was present. Last time, others had designed it. Her wedding. And she'd let them.

This time, she hadn't.

And she felt it now. The room was not a display for others to enjoy.

It was personal.

It was for *them*.

Had she known even then, weeks ago, distracting herself with these plans, she was in love?

She'd been protecting herself, hadn't she?

Protecting herself from all that lived inside her.

It had always lived there, she realised now.

Every day, since she'd confessed it to herself, the day she'd let the bud of it sprout, it had bloomed.

It flooded through her like a tidal wave.

It couldn't be stopped.

She couldn't build a dam.

Love. All-consuming. She carried it with her. She carried love. In her heart. In her soul.

She loved him.

Konstantinos.

Her feet stooped beneath the arch.

When she was young, she'd thought love fixed everything. But she understood now, standing here, that love was a complicated thing.

It could hurt.

It hurt her now, knowing when she stood here in three days' time, when she met him here, she'd have to wrap them both in her love, because his love…

He didn't know how to let it bloom.

He was afraid of it. *Its intensity.*

But she saw it now. Every day.

He loved her.

He always had.

He'd yanked her into his world. He'd done everything he could to keep her safe—to keep her with him.

Was *that* not love?

It wasn't a fairy-tale love.

It was *his* love.

And she knew she had to accept it.

He'd never be ready to confess it.

She couldn't force him.

It wasn't something she could explain or teach.

He had to do *that* on his own. *Feel it.* Just as he had to accept his grief.

Her heart, although it was full of love, it still ached.

Ached with the knowledge that she could never tell him the truth. Everything was to go back to how it was before. He wanted that, and she'd promised it.

She closed her eyes.

After the ceremony, he was still going away. He'd go back to his meetings—back to work.

She'd wait for him here. With her love she could never give him openly.

'*Glikia mou.*'

Her eyes opened.

She turned.

Between the open doors, he stood. At the opposite end of the aisle, he wasn't in a suit. He wore jeans and a white T-shirt. He was dressed for no one's eyes but hers.

Her beautiful husband.

Her heart roared. It was ready. Ready to burst free and land at his feet.

She swallowed. Waited for him as he walked towards her. His eyes only on her and hers only on him.

And there they met at the altar. Beneath the arch of flowers, and her heart, it ached. Ached that when they really did this, it wouldn't be for them. It would be for his image.

But *this*, this moment, could be for them.

She could reconfirm her vows today.

And she knew she'd mean every word.

Poppy didn't speak. Too afraid the words in her throat, her confessions of love, would spill into his ears, and he'd turn away from her, walk back down the aisle without her. Leave her and her love behind.

A tremble raked through her.

He frowned. His dark eyes probing.

But she couldn't let him see.

She wouldn't make him afraid.

'Poppy?'

She shook her head. Reached for him. Placed her palm to his bristled cheek. She leaned in. Brushed her mouth against his.

She kissed him.

Kissed him with all of her love.

And she promised with her lips—her mouth—she'd love him. *Always*.

Her love would always be his.

It always was.

She thrust her fingers into his hair—her fingers—her hands—moving to cradle his nape.

She could do this, she told herself.

Her love *would* be strong enough for both of them.

Konstantinos could do nothing but accept her kiss. The intensity of it. It was the same as their every kiss, an explosion, but this was…*different*.

She drank from his mouth as if it was their first kiss, but somehow their last. As if it were a goodbye, but also hello.

His chest tightened.

He didn't understand it. These thoughts in his head. And so he ignored them. These things he didn't understand.

He pushed his fingers into her hair and met her intensity with his own with the sweep of his tongue. The pressure of his lips.

And then her hands were on his chest. Her palms pushing, she pulled her lips from his.

He didn't want her to pull away.

He wanted her close.

He swallowed. Opened his eyes. Met the blue of hers.

'After the ceremony,' he growled, because he needed to tell her. This decision, he realised, he'd made. Right now. *Here*. In the chapel. 'I'll stay here with you.'

She blinked. 'What about work?'

'If I must leave, you'll come with me.'

And he knew that was how it would be between them now. She would be with him. *Always*.

'Yes,' she breathed. 'I'll be with you. Wherever *you* are.'

His heart galloped.

Her kiss hadn't been a hello or a goodbye.

It wasn't a first or a last.

It was a promise.

A promise that she was here with him.

He'd promise the same.

'*We* will be together.'

CHAPTER FIFTEEN

Three Days Later...

Poppy fingered the flowers that made up the bodice of her dress. She hadn't thought they'd pull it off in time, this design of hers. A wedding dress made of flowers. But they had. A dress she'd designed for herself. Designed for him to see her in it.

And here she stood, wearing it.

Her stomach cramped.

She placed her palm there, to the hurt. Closed her eyes. Shut out the eyes looking back at her from the three large ornate mirrors reflecting them from each angled surface.

Her reflection knew what she tried to hide from.

Her reflection remembered what it felt like to carry a secret.

It was heavy.

It was pain.

Oh, it had hurt the little girl she'd been to look at her mother every day and withhold the truth.

Did she really think she could do it again? Look at Konstantinos every day and hide this secret?

Today, standing in front of all of them, it would be a lie. A lie she would be promising to keep.

It would make *her* a liar for the rest of her life. If she did this today there would be no going back on her lie—her promise—to maintain the marriage they'd had.

They didn't have the marriage they'd had. They were closer. She was…

She loved him.

She should have trusted her mother to do the right thing for both of them if she'd told her the truth about her dad.

She *did* trust Konstantinos.

She trusted him to do the right thing.

For them *both*.

She had to tell him the truth before they married and were held together by the secret she would have to keep hidden for the rest of her life.

Her love.

She opened her eyes; met the older eyes of the woman she'd become in the mirror.

She didn't want to be the little girl she'd been.

She didn't want to live on a knife's edge that one day what she hid would be discovered.

She should have told her mum.

She should have been brave.

The cramps eased in her stomach.

She stood tall. Straightened her spine.

She had to tell him the truth.

It was an invasion.

Konstantinos pushed his hands inside the pockets of his trousers and surveyed the army of ants beneath his window. They *were* fire ants, in too big tiaras and gowns of silk. They herded together dressed in costume. Reds and oranges, blacks and blues. They left their boats at the jetty, landed in rows on the helipad, and in they swarmed.

He was surrounded from every angle. The island was being taken over by select journalists, celebrities, dignitaries, and business associates.

He'd invited them to gather. To attack as one. To bite. To nip at the bubble he'd trapped them in. Him and her. And now they were tearing it apart. Intruding on the life he'd hidden himself in for weeks with Poppy. *Just them*. And this…

He knew why today was important. He understood the stakes, but he didn't want them here. He didn't want to parade in front of them. He didn't want to make *her* stand in front of them.

Poppy's shuttered looks had happened more often these last few days. Her eyes had stared too long at him. And the kiss in the chapel…

She's hiding something from you.

She wasn't.

She was worried about today.

He snarled at them. Bared his teeth.

He wanted them to see. To be here and bear witness to the strength of the marriage they had probed in the press. He hadn't wanted them to receive a carefully organised selection of photographs; even the best photographs could be distorted by a journalist who wasn't in attendance. And the distortion would be classed as free speech—an opinion.

He wanted them all to know the facts. *See them*. They were strong. His marriage was strong.

But it was a violation. *He* felt violated. And he couldn't explain it. He'd invited them!

His hands balled into fists in his pockets.

What was wrong with him?

All his life, he'd fought to project the right image. Of the right kind of man. But none of it felt…*important*.

He turned on his heel and made his way to the door.

He'd get this over with. *Now.*

Afterwards, everything would go back to how it was before.

He reached for the handle.

The handle was torn from his grasp.

The door opened outwards.

Flowers. Tiny white blooms, some closed buds, with the smallest green leaves, some open, made up the bodice of her dress to her waist. And then, like ivy, the flowers snaked down her hips. Sheer organza silk flared there. Made up her layered skirts to fall to her feet. Her silk pumps. *More flowers*. As if she took the world with her wherever she went. Her footsteps cushioned by uncrushable petals.

'Is it not bad luck,' he asked thickly, 'for the groom to see the bride before the wedding?'

'We're already married,' she said, half turning, and closing the door.

He noted the twitch of her fingers. He tensed. 'What is it?'

'Konstantinos, I...'

His black gaze narrowed, burrowed inside the blue of hers. 'Tell me what it is?'

Poppy looked at him. He was immaculate. His every hair combed to perfection. His grey morning suit, it all fit him like a second skin. She didn't want to corner him. She didn't want to fight. But it made her sick.

All these lies.

'Konstantinos—' she dragged in a breath until it fortified the walls of her lungs '—I can't do it.'

'Can't do what?'

'I can't go out there.'

The pulse in his clean-shaven jaw ticked. 'You are nervous?'

'No.' She shook her head. 'Not of them.'

'Then of whom?'

She bit her lip. She *was* nervous of the cameras—*the eyes*—but that wasn't why she wasn't going out there.

'I'm nervous about telling you the truth.'

He cocked a brow. 'The truth?'

'It's a risk,' she said. 'I know that now. I knew it when I was a girl. That's why I never said it. I never told her. My mum. I made myself believe I was happy. Happy for my father to just be there. But I'm not happy, Konstantinos. I'm not happy to live a lie just because it's easier any more.'

Dark brows drew together. 'Who is telling lies here, *agape*?'

'*Me*,' she confessed, and she felt it. Something lifting from her shoulders. Easing the pressure from her heart. 'I know if I tell you the truth it could ruin everything. But…' Flashes of being all alone without him, of learning to sleep alone, of missing him tore through her. 'I have to tell you.'

'Poppy—'

'*Please*,' she interrupted. 'I can't… I can't keep lying. Putting on a show. All my life, I've put on a show for others. I've lied again and again. And if I go out there, I'll still be a liar. I'll be lying to you, because it wouldn't be a show for me.' Air, too shallow, stuttered in between her tight lips. 'It will be real for *me*.'

He stepped back. 'What do you mean?'

'I want a real marriage. A marriage we both deserve to have. A marriage with all the foundations we promised to each other. Loyalty, protection, *and* love, Konstantinos. We can have love, too.'

'I don't want *that*,' he growled. 'I never did.'

Poppy searched his eyes, his facial features, but there was nothing. Not a frown, not a dip of his lips. He was pretending as if what she'd said hadn't touched him. But she knew him now. She knew how well he'd taught himself to hide his emotions. Control them. But underneath the veneer he'd taught himself to hide behind, he was—

'You're scared.'

'I'm not scared,' he countered, his voice too stiff, too barren of anything.

He wouldn't fool her now. She didn't believe it. His indifference.

'I'm scared, too,' she admitted. 'I've always been scared.

Scared to trust you. I was scared you'd betray me like my father. But I don't want to be scared any more. I trust you. I know we'd never hurt each other on purpose… What happened before. We couldn't help it. I understand why. Our parents. But I'm not them and neither are you. We get to choose now. We get to have this. We deserve it, Konstantinos, to have the family neither of us had with each other. Together. You and me.'

She inched closer, craning her neck to keep hold of his eyes. 'I love you, Konstantinos,' she said, and she waited, her heart beating so hard, so fast, for him to say he loved her back. But he didn't speak. He looked at her. Regarding her with a wide-eyed contemplation.

He closed the minimal space between them. 'How pretty you make it all sound.' His hand rose. He cradled her cheek. 'This *love* of yours. This *life* you want to give *me*.'

So desperately did she want to lean into the heat of it. But his touch, however softly he held her there, it felt off. Something wasn't right.

She ignored it. Her instincts. She'd make him understand.

'We can build it together,' she told him thickly. 'A new life. Without rules… A *real* fresh start.'

He dipped his head. 'You say you love me?'

'More than anything.'

'And this love, it will protect those you profess to love. It will protect me?'

'*Yes!*'

His lips turned upwards, but it wasn't a smile. It was all teeth and the movement of lips. But it was…*vicious*.

Lower his head came.

Closer his lips.

'*Liar*,' he breathed into her mouth.

Poppy flinched. '*What?*'

His hand fell from her cheek. He raised his head. Brought himself to his full height before her. 'It must be so hard, after your father, to differentiate when your truth is nothing but another lie.'

'*Konstantinos!*' she hissed, because his words—his accusation she was telling lies… It scrambled her thoughts. Stole her conviction she *was* telling the truth.

He turned his back on her. 'You are a liar, Poppy,' he said again, walking over to his desk, opening a drawer.

She squared her shoulders. Ignored her instincts to turn tail and run. Something brewed in the air between them. *Conflict.* She could smell it. *Taste it.*

She planted her feet. She wasn't running this time because of her fear.

'I'm not lying.'

'But you are,' he said, and slipped free a Manila folder. He closed the drawer, walked to his high-back chair made of dark wood. He pulled it out. Sat down. And only then did he look at her.

'Your love is no better than my mother's or my father's.'

'They didn't love you.'

'*Exactly.* My mother, she abandoned me because she was selfish. My father abandoned my mother and me because he was selfish. You are selfish, too, Poppy. Only thinking of what you want—what *you* need.'

'I'm thinking of what we both need.'

'What will you do if I do not return your love?'

'I—'

'You'll leave me standing at the altar. You will abandon me. *Again. That* is not love.'

'How do you know what love is if you've never felt it? I know what love is, Konstantinos. *This* is love. I love you. You love me.'

'I loved my mother and she died, because my love was selfish, too. I should have called for help, but my heart demanded I follow her. *Save her.*'

The navy-blue walls surrounding them—the blue of the sea at his back—it all swirled. Closed in on her like storm clouds.

'You weren't to blame, Konstantinos,' she said, it all becoming clear in her head. His need for control. How he was twisting everything now so he was in charge of the narrative.

'Your mother's death wasn't your fault. You had no control over her choice, Konstantinos. You can't control everything. Others' actions. I couldn't control my dad's.'

'*This has nothing to do with my mother!*'

'But it does,' she realised out loud. 'It's why you couldn't admit you loved Isaak.'

'You will not bring him into this,' he warned darkly.

'You love him, don't you? You just can't let it out. These feelings. All this love, because it makes you feel out of control. Like it did in the sea with your mother.'

His dark eyes blazed. 'I am always in control.'

'You can't be, Konstantinos. You *must* realise that now. After your mum, Isaak—*me*. Life happens. Some things are out of our control. But they happen. Bad things. *Horrible things*. And we can either let them break us, or we let them strengthen us. And this—' she waved at the entirety of him '—pretending nothing affects you—that you feel nothing—is…' She didn't want to call him weak. He was the strongest man she'd ever met. 'It's not strong, Konstantinos,' she finished.

His shoulders squared. 'I am not *weak*.'

'You don't want to admit you love me. You don't want to risk having a *real* marriage, because you loved your mother, and she abandoned you in the worst way possible. I'll never abandon you when things are hard. I'll be there for you. *Always*. I will never put you in second place again,' she promised.

He glared at her. 'You just did.'

'I…' Doubt pressed against her temples. '*No*.'

'You want this,' he told her. 'Not *me*.'

'You want this. I know it.'

He shook his head. 'You want to believe that, because it is what *you* want.'

'You're frightened—'

'Everything I have done,' he pressed, his voice hard as steel, 'our marriage, the last few weeks, was to make you play a part. A part I wanted you to play. I got in your head. I made you think you were safe to let down your guard. I made you believe you could trust me.'

'I *do* trust you.'

'Then you are a fool. I cannot be trusted. I am a liar, too, Poppy, but I am more skilled than you at it. You do not know me.'

'I know you more now than I ever did,' she said, because it was the truth. She knew him now. Knew herself.

'You only know what I have let you know,' he said. 'I am not fair. I am not…*considerate*.'

'You're all those things,' she said. '*More*.'

'I am a fake,' he countered. 'I am selfish. I care for nothing. No one. Only myself. And I won't hide from the ugliness of the truth. I am my father's son.'

'You are Konstantinos Ariti. You are loyal. You are a protector. Your father was never those things. He left you all alone to take care of your sick mother. *You* would never do that. You didn't do that to me. You made sure I was safe.'

'I always meant to hurt you, Poppy.'

'Not on purpose,' she almost shouted.

'I did,' he contradicted. 'I will never give you the opportunity to humiliate me again.' He dipped his head to the page in front of him. Added a word to the front page.

His signature.

Her heart dropped to her stomach. 'What are you signing?'

He flicked to another page, and another, adding his signature. 'The divorce papers.'

She couldn't breathe.

'You will sign the papers.' He held out his pen. '*Now.*'

'No.'

'You will sign them,' he repeated. 'And you will leave.'

'I'm not going anywhere.'

'When I found you,' he said. 'The contract. The sex. The divorce. When you demanded we find closure…' He placed the pen on the table. Leant forward, his arms on the edge of the desk. Oh, so nonchalantly. 'I agreed to it all, and do you know why, Poppy?'

Her heart pounded. '*Why?*'

'Revenge.'

'*Revenge?*'

'Retribution, for your abandonment. For shattering the image I had worked all my life to project,' he clarified. 'I did it so when you needed me,' his nostrils flared, 'I'd send you away.'

'That's not true.'

'I have manipulated you from the very beginning. I have tricked you, Poppy. *Deceived you.*'

'You're lying.'

'Why would I lie now? It's over. The façade. So why would I keep pretending?'

'*Pretending?*'

'I've been toying with you.'

'The contract. I know…' she said. 'We were both fighting for control, but it was always going to end this way. I know that, and so do you. We love each other.'

'I have never, and will never love *you.*'

Her knees wobbled. She felt weak. *Sick.* Had it all been a lie?

She'd put her love out there, asked for his in return, and he had made it something ugly. *Selfish.*

He picked up the pen. Held it out to her. His hand didn't tremble. His fingers pure stone, he held it there as if nothing was going on beneath his skin. As if he felt nothing.

'Sign it, Poppy.'

CHAPTER SIXTEEN

Konstantinos watched her fight them down. Tears intended to bring him closer. Intended to make him react.

He wouldn't.

He'd let her in. Beneath his skin. She'd got into his head. He'd been ready to walk away from today, because he'd wanted to protect *her*. But she was never going to do it, anyway. Renew their vows. She'd planned *this* all along. To subdue him with her *honesty*. To leave him up there—*alone*—at the altar.

He'd given her ammunition. Told her where she could wound him most. He'd told her things he'd told no one. He'd given her the bullets, and she'd brought the gun. Loaded it while he watched. She'd shot him with words of *love*.

She's not trying to kill you.

But she was. *He knew.*

Love was a weakness. It was why his mother had never loved him. Because if she had loved him, she never would have walked into the sea. She never would have abandoned him. She never would have put him second best to her depression, or to the hate she felt for his father. She never would have left him behind. If he had not loved his mother, he would have stayed on the shore. He would not have fought against the tide to save her. He would have called for help—for larger arms. But he'd been weak. His love—*his panic*—had let her drown. Because love was a selfish emotion.

'Sign it,' he demanded again, and he caught it too late. The fire heating his demand.

A tear dripped from her chin. 'Where do I need to sign?' She walked over to the desk, faced him from the other side, and took the pen from his fingers. She reached for the papers. Her fingers trembling. '*Here?*' she asked, turning the document to face her. 'Only on the front page?'

'And pages two, three and six,' he confirmed, grateful for the barrier between them. Grateful he didn't have to stand close. Grateful he couldn't smell her now. Because it would make him ill, he assured himself. A scent he'd always thought of as *hers*.

The pen hovered above the first box.

Her eyes flitted over the page.

She wiped at her nose with the back of her hand. Ducked her head and signed all the pages.

She closed the document. Slid it over to him.

'What happens next?'

'My lawyer will have it in the hour,' he said. 'As we are both Greek citizens and our divorce is by mutual consent, it could take a few weeks. *I* will ensure it is less.'

She didn't look at him again. She stood. Walked away from him and reached for the door—

'Poppy?'

She turned, and it flashed in her eyes. He recognised it. *Hope.* Hope this had all been a terrible mistake.

It wasn't.

He'd crush the light in her eyes.

Just as she had intended to crush *him*.

'Don't forget this,' he said, and reached into the drawer again. He held it out for her to collect. A single piece of paper.

She walked back over to him and put her hand out for it. Her gaze dipped. 'What is it?'

'It's Léon's debt.'

She clasped it on one end whilst he held the other.

Their eyes locked over it.

'I keep my promises,' he reminded her. 'Unlike you.'

Her face fell.

'Goodbye, Poppy.'

He pushed himself to his feet. Turned his back on her and walked to the window. Watched the display of new arrivals. New ants. All too bright. All too…*fake*. None of it was real. Not out there. Not in here. She was right. It was all a show.

A lie.

He closed his eyes. He didn't need to open his eyes to know she moved closer. He felt her there. Behind him. *Too close.* Her stature was so small compared to his height. His build. But how largely her presence overshadowed him. Oh, so floral was her scent. Only hers. Only ever Poppy's.

It overwhelmed him now.

His heart, he hated it. How it pumped, *harder*. Responded to her even now.

'Goodbye, Konstantinos.'

The clink of metal on wood pierced his eardrums. *Her rings.*

No longer did his heart hammer. It stopped beating. His lungs, they froze. But his ears, oversensitised, they listened to her light footsteps as she turned. The ruffle of her silk skirts. He heard the door open. Heard her pause.

The silence pulsed.

The lock clicked.

His fingers went to his throat. He yanked free the knot. But still he could not breathe.

He thudded to his knees. Placed his hands on the floor, palm-side down.

He wasn't hyperventilating. His body, it was responding to the near-fatal attack of his wife.

He was in control.

He sucked in air through his nostrils—exhaled through his mouth.

Then why did his heart hurt?

Why could he not breathe?

Why did this feel like…*death*?

Anger quickened Poppy's step through the corridor with a too high ceiling and too many windows. Too many streaks of sunlight glared into her eyes. Made the tears she held back blur her vision.

He'd had no intention of starting again.

He was the liar.

He'd lied about stopping the games.

He'd dismissed her as if she were no one.

She reached out, steadied herself with each step against the wall.

She should have trusted her instincts and run away the minute she'd felt something was wrong. Because now *everything* was wrong. Nothing was the way it should be. But at least now she knew.

He'd let her get close. He'd let her open herself up to him. He'd let her fall in love with him. And he'd known he was always going to send her away.

He was worse than her father.

He was a monster.

She moved down the corridor to the lift.

She hit the button to call it. *Repeatedly.* Watched the sundial above its doors move. Oh, so slowly, it climbed upwards to where she was. On the top floor.

No one would come up here, on this side of the monastery. They'd all be in the chapel on the hill. *Waiting.* But the urgency to get out, to leave, it pulsed through her. She needed out. Off the island. She needed to be far away from him. And maybe then it would stop hurting.

It didn't before.

She looked down at the crumpled document in her hand. She smoothed it out against her thigh.

She blinked away the mist, looked back down the corridor of green walls to the oak door and iron hinges, locking her out here. On the outside.

A muffled sound ripped free from her mouth.

Flashes of Konstantinos at Isaak's grave tore through her. The sound his mouth had made. So raw. *That* had been real.

The lift doors opened. She walked inside, her chest heaving. She collapsed against the back wall.

Her heart cracked.

The tears didn't trickle.

They spilt down her cheeks in waves.

A sob tore free from her throat.

He'd retreated behind his walls of control. He'd twisted her love until it became something ugly. *Selfish betrayal.* She hadn't meant to betray him. She…

He *had* stopped playing games. He'd fallen in love with her, too. But how could she expect him to give her what he'd never had?

The doors closed.

It was too late to change her mind now.

She'd messed it all up.

She was quivering. *Shaking.* Tears rolled down her cheeks. It raked through her. Emotion after breathtaking emotion.

She didn't fight it.

She cried for him. For her. For Isaak. She cried for the happily-ever-after they could have had, but their pasts had stolen it. But most of all, Poppy cried for all the words said too late to save their marriage.

It was over.

CHAPTER SEVENTEEN

Twelve Days Later...

KONSTANTINOS HELD THE final divorce decree in his hand.

For twelve days, he'd been waiting for this. Expedited it under Greek law. For his marriage to be stamped void. *Over.* For the document in his hand to ease the pressure on his lungs—to let him breathe. But still, he couldn't draw breath deep enough. Still, he walked. He'd been walking every day, visited every hermitage on the island. And he couldn't find it. *Air.*

He hadn't left the island.

He hadn't checked the press.

He hadn't looked for *her*.

His lungs squeezed.

He was all alone. The island was his self-imposed prison. He understood *this* was what he deserved now.

Forever second best.

Forever abandoned.

He was to be forever alone.

His step quickened. He didn't know where he was going. Where he'd end up. It was the same every day. Through the trees and over the clifftops he walked. He searched for what the island promised. What the monks had called it when they had made it their home so long ago.

Salvation.

The trees rustled.

He stopped. Looked down at what they guarded.

His son.

He wasn't alone on the island.

Tentacles slithered. He didn't cut them down at the root. He let them drop him to his knees. Let them squeeze out whatever air remained in his lungs. And on his knees, Konstantinos remained. Looking at the white headstone. At his name.

Isaak Ariti.

The pain in his gut doubled him over.

Pain. It followed him. It was his punishment. For letting his mother die. And so *they*—the gods, the fates, whatever stood jury and executioner above him in a world he could not see, but knew was there—had taken Isaak to punish him. And in turn he had hurt her.

Konstantinos didn't fight it. He lay down on the neat grass. Lay down with him. His son. He touched the tiny flowers placed in the vase. Wild flowers. Pink. Purple. Blue.

He'd failed them all, because however hard he'd tried to protect them, he hadn't been able to.

'I'm sorry,' he breathed heavily. He reached out—traced the gold-embossed letters. 'I'm sorry I couldn't protect you.'

It hit him. *Grief.* Thick and overwhelming, it cloaked him. A visceral darkness that pummelled his every sense. It was everything he remembered, this grief. It choked him, as it had the day he'd held his mother in his arms…

Konstantinos let it take him.

Emotions—so many of them—thumped at his skin—his body.

This grief, it was real.

Isaak…

He was real.

A tear slipped free.

Konstantinos let it fall.

His son deserved his tears.

He deserved his father to recognise him.

Because denying his grief—it was denying his existence.

'I waited for you to breathe,' he told his son. 'I didn't believe them. I did not believe you could be given to me and taken away before I had time to do it right. Protect you. Raise you. *Love you.*'

His chest split in half. 'I pretended I didn't care. I pretended I had not touched your small toes. Your fingers. I pretended the box I carried here was empty. I am sorry I denied you. You are my son, Isaak. My first born…'

He sat up. Kissed the white stone. 'I am sorry I did not grieve for you. I love you,' he whispered. 'And your mother, she—she loves you.'

He closed his eyes.

God, forgive him.

What had he done?

He'd denied his grief. He had not let her have hers. Because he had told her their baby—his death—was nothing. He had denied her grief. He had denied her love. And why? For control?

His chest caught fire. And he knew what burnt inside him. It was ferocious, so hot did it burn. It hurt him. He knew why it hurt now. Why it had hurt when she'd disappeared. Why he'd stopped everything to find her. Why he'd demanded she stay. Why he'd played all those games to keep her. It was not for his image. Or his reputation.

He loved his wife.

Konstantinos understood it now.

He understood everything.

So unafraid was she of her feelings. To let them take her. She was strong. Strong in ways he couldn't be. Would never let himself be. Because he'd seen what *feeling* could do. His mother, she'd felt too much. She could not compartmentalise. And it had destroyed her.

He would not let himself be destroyed by…*emotion.*

He would not let himself…*feel*.

And yet, he *felt*.

His skin ached as if he had the flu.

His throat was scraped raw.

Bile rose in his mouth. He'd used mind games. Manipulated her. Turned her honesty—her vulnerability—into a weapon. Turned her love against her.

He didn't know how to fix what he'd done…

Poppy, she deserved more.

She deserved to know the truth.

He owed her *that*.

He owed Isaak too.

Forty-Eight Hours Later…

'To new beginnings.'

Poppy looked at Léon's raised glass. The deep red wine within it. Her feet curled beneath her on the sofa, she shifted her bottom forward so she could reach his outstretched glass from where he sat in his wheelchair beside her. She raised her glass. Silently, she clinked it to his.

'It will ease,' he said, taking a sip. 'Time—it's a strange thing, Poppy. It lets us…*heal*. Never fully, but it changes us,' he said, and she wanted to oppose his statement.

Time, it did nothing but turn pain into a numbness. But she was never without it. It just changed form. *Grief.* There was no medicine for it. No surgery to cut it out.

'It opens us to the *possibility* of change,' he continued. 'Soon you'll see, *this*, your divorce, *is* a new beginning.'

She smiled. She understood he knew grief. She knew he'd opened his home to her again as his friend. She knew tonight he'd told them to set the fire alight to warm her as he had every night since she'd been here. She knew he understood she didn't want to be alone, so he sat with her when the night closed in. When her loneliness was most acute. When still she missed him.

Konstantinos had been generous in the settlement. The Paris apartment was hers. It had been hers from the moment she'd left the island. The lawyer had contacted the lawyer appointed for her by Konstantinos.

She was sure there were implications there of her ex-husband providing her with legal counsel. But she understood he hadn't wanted to talk to her. And she hadn't been ready to talk to him. She hadn't wanted anything from him. She hadn't needed legal representation, yet he'd ensured she had enough money to be financially secure forever. The island they would share, because of Isaak. He required forty-eight hours' notice if she wanted to go and he'd accommodate her, and it was expected she'd do the same for him.

It was all fair.

All wrapped up with neat little bows.

It was over. Their separation was official. Unofficially, in the secret place inside her heart…it would never be over. She didn't know what to do with that. There was no closure incoming. There was only the regret of what-ifs.

Tomorrow, maybe the next day, or the next, she'd figure it out. But right now, she just wanted to sit with it. *Feel it.* The loss of what could have been. She wasn't scared these feelings would take her under. She'd been under, and she'd made it out. She was a survivor, and she'd keep on surviving. One day, maybe she'd learn how to thrive. But today, tomorrow… she was okay to just…*be.*

She took a sip of her wine.

The lounge was a beautiful room. Not one where visitors were allowed. This was the place where Léon had spent time with his family, doing all the things normal families did. It hurt her to be in here with him. It filled her full of yearning, but it also stroked something inside her. Made her hunker down into the plush cushions of the sofa.

It made her…*warm*.

'A little TV, I think…' Léon reached for the remote.

Poppy half turned and placed her glass on the tall table of oak. 'Sounds good.'

The TV was cleverly disguised as an ornate gold mirror, so the pretty moving pictures were not the focal point. So in this room conversations could happen. Books could be taken from the shelves. Stories could be shared.

Poppy had no more stories. Books—she couldn't concentrate long enough. And so it had become a kind of ritual. To fill the silence with a hum, while they just sat together. Sometimes they talked. Sometimes they didn't.

The reflective glass changed to an image.

Two chairs sat opposite each other on the screen. It resembled a lounge, with cream rugs and armchairs. Poppy knew this show. *Anna Talks*.

Anna walked onto the stage. Her suit as neutral as the set. Beige. Hands waving at a crowd the camera zoomed out to capture as they all applauded her. Poppy liked this show. She liked how at first it seemed frivolous. Just moving pictures, celebrities, politicians, on some kind of promotional tour. But Anna, her questions were always so simple, but they got responses no one expected.

A live show, it wasn't rehearsed or scripted. She went deeper. Beyond the interviewee's public status. She brought her guests to life. Showed the human beneath their too bright smiles.

It was escapist TV. She got to focus on someone else's life— *their problems*—rather than her own.

Anna took her seat. 'Today we welcome a tycoon who has been in the press for numerous reasons.' Her eyes sparkled at the camera, as if she knew a secret and so did the audience. They chuckled.

'He's won many prestigious awards for his due diligence in the workplace for mental health. And most recently, his personal life. Never before has he given an interview… Please, let us welcome—' she raised her hands, turned her attention to the obscured glass doors that would welcome her guest '—Mr Konstantinos Ariti!'

Poppy's blood roared. It drowned out the applause booming as the doors opened. He didn't smile. He didn't wave back at the audience. He walked towards his host, and sat down in the chair designated for him.

He wasn't dressed in a suit. He was…*casual*. Dark blue jeans, a round-necked black jumper. His hair, it curled around his ears. His usually clean-shaven cheeks hidden behind a beard.

Anna stretched her hand out. 'Welcome.'

Konstantinos did the same. 'Thank you for having me, Anna.'

Their hands fell.

Poppy's heart raced as she watched Anna do what she did with every guest. She paused for a little too long. She looked at her guest as if she saw them. Saw beneath whatever script they usually gave to their host, and she was waiting for them to forget it. Their rehearsed words. To forget their lies and give her only the truth.

'How are you, Konstantinos?' she asked.

He didn't move. Konstantinos sat there as still as stone, absorbing her question. 'I want,' he said, and he paused.

The tiny pause, the tiny hesitation, it made Poppy's heart pump.

'I want,' he said again, 'to tell you I'm okay, Anna.'

'But you're not?'

'No.'

Anna didn't push. Didn't ask him why not. She waited.

And so did Poppy.

'I am sad, Anna.'

'And it's important for you to tell us this? *Why?*'

'The truth,' he said, 'it is power, and for so long I have not been truthful. I've said the right words. Won awards for teaching others it is okay *not* to be okay.'

'And why was that important for you to do?'

'My mother.' He swallowed. 'She wasn't well. She was… mentally ill. She took her own life because no one reached out to help her. Not my father. He thought her sickness was a weakness. He locked her away from the public when her health deteriorated. He left her with me. Trusted me to take care of her.'

'Do you blame yourself for your mother's death, Konstantinos?'

'I couldn't protect her.'

'How do you think you failed her?'

'I… I wasn't a strong swimmer. I panicked,' he admitted. 'She drowned.'

'Her death,' she said. 'It made you believe you had to save everyone? *Protect them?*'

'Yes.' His teeth gritted. 'I grew up, Anna, believing it was my job to protect everyone. I created an environment where *my* people knew *I* would look after them. They were not scared to ask for help.'

'Are *you* asking for help now?'

Konstantinos's jaw turned to granite. 'All my life, I never asked for help.' His fingers curled around the ends of the armrests.

Anna stayed silent. Let the weight of Konstantinos's words hang in the air. Until everyone felt it. The unbearable weight on his shoulders.

A broken sound fell from Poppy's lips.

'My father was a man who did not allow for weakness,' he explained. 'Image was everything. His reputation… He was in control of all things. He *kept* control of everything in any way he could. He taught me to do the same. To be strong. I was taught emotion was weakness. I had to bury my—my feelings. Or…'

'*Or?*' The single-worded question was soft, not demanding. It encouraged Konstantinos—the audience—to believe it was just him and her. The talk show a safe place to confess. *Everything*.

'If I let myself feel…if I let myself cry—*grieve*—for my mother…it would make me weak. And weakness was death. When my son died, I did the same. I did not cry. I did not grieve. I was everything I was taught to be. *Strong*—' His voice broke and so did something inside Poppy.

'I'm sorry you lost your mother, Konstantinos.'

'I am, too,' he said thickly.

'And your son,' she added. 'I can't imagine. I'm so sorry.'

Poppy held her breath.

'I pretended his death meant nothing,' he admitted roughly. 'But it was…*everything*. It took the separation from my wife for me to realise how much pain I was in.'

Tension corded his throat.

It curled around her heart and held it. *His slip*. He'd called her his wife, not his ex.

It wasn't over for him, either.

Anna caught it too.

'Your wife?' she asked, so gently did she guide him.

'Poppy,' he said.

'Tell us about her?'

'I hurt her,' he confessed. 'My inability to grieve. To feel… I wanted to be strong for her. Strong in all the ways I hadn't been able to be for my mother. I needed to protect my wife. But I couldn't stop Isaak from dying. I could not take away her grief. And, however illogical, I blamed myself for the death of our son. I blamed myself for my wife's grief. *Her pain*.'

'Do you still blame yourself?'

'I will work through this, Anna, with a therapist.' Lips compressed, Konstantinos shook his head. 'But I understand now, to confront the irrationality of my thoughts I need to be honest. I am not okay, Anna. I am grieving. *Deeply*. For my mother. For my son. For the end of my marriage. I am grieving for the marriage I could have had.'

Anna didn't hit him with a follow-up. She waited for him to carry on, to tell his truth and for the world to hear him. To see this powerful man own his feelings. His mistakes. His regret. *His grief.*

And it was powerful. Poppy could feel it inside *that* studio. Inside the room with her.

'Poppy, she is stronger than I could ever be. She isn't afraid to feel. She is not afraid to let the world know how deeply she does. She does not care about image or reputations. *She loves.* And to love is sometimes pain, but it's the root of everything… *good.* I want to do good in the world,' he told Anna. 'I want my son's—Isaak's—death to change me for the better. I want to feel all the things I have never let myself feel. I want to grieve. I want the world to know I—I love him.'

He closed his eyes.

The camera zoomed in.

Poppy wanted to reach through the screen—drag him into her arms. *Hold him.*

He opened his eyes. So dark, so black. *So vulnerable.*

He looked into the camera. And she felt he looked at her. *Only her.*

'I love my wife.'

The camera zoomed out.

'I know you have something to share with us,' Anna said. 'Would you like to share that now?'

'I would.' Konstantinos swallowed. 'Going live tomorrow is a new foundation. The Ariti Group will be funding it. *I* will fund it,' he corrected. 'It is called Isaak's Foundation. It is for those who have lost—for those who still love. It will help fami-

lies stay together in their grief. It will give them the tools to…
to grieve. It will be Isaak's legacy.'

The crowd burst into applause.

Poppy stood. Her mind buzzed with too many incoherent
thoughts. Too many threads she couldn't connect. He'd gone
on telly and shattered his reputation. The image he wanted everyone to believe. That he was unbreakable.

He was breaking right there on the television. He was grieving. Allowing himself to admit their baby was someone. His
death meant something. It meant something to him. And she
wasn't with him. She was not there. Holding his hand. *Holding him.*

She should never have left the island.

She should have stayed and just been there. *For him.*

He loved her.

'The car is waiting for you outside.'

'*What?*' she breathed. She'd forgotten about Léon.

'The car will take you to him.'

Her heart raced.

'It's a live recording near to here. Save your marriage, Poppy.
Family, it is all we have. All that matters. Love him. Let him
love you.'

Love. It was all she ever wanted.

She leant down and kissed Léon's cheek.

He reached for her hand. Squeezed it. 'Go,' he said. '*Now.*'

Poppy ran.

CHAPTER EIGHTEEN

Konstantinos was shattered.

Internally, it was as if everything was shredded. Ripped apart. And they could all see it. He was exposed. *He* had exposed himself. And yet, he didn't feel vulnerable. He did not feel weak before all those eyes now watching him leave his dressing room.

He almost felt…*reborn*.

He hadn't gone on the show as a businessman. He'd left behind his suit. He had gone as a man. A husband. A father. *A son.* And he hoped if there was a little boy out there watching him, he understood what he hadn't when he was a child. Not even when he was a man.

There were different types of strength.

Poppy had shown him that. That to feel, it wasn't always nice. It wasn't always easy. But it was the truth. Truth was power. It was strength. To feel, to sit with those feelings, however hard they were—it was what living was.

He had not been living for so long. He'd convinced himself his strength differed from his father's. But it hadn't been different. He had been out of control, just like his father, running away from anything…*real.* Squashed it as if it wasn't important.

Somewhere inside him, he'd known all along that facing his emotions—*his feelings*—was the only way to move forward. To be his best self. He'd preached it for years to his staff. He'd got help for his wife. But he could not help himself.

Today, it was for Isaak. It was in part for Poppy. But he'd done it for himself. He was done lying. He was done pretending he didn't feel.

He thanked his son for that. For waiting for him. For showing him he could lie down. He could let himself rest. He could let himself...*feel*.

He thanked her too. For loving him—for trying to get him to open himself to love.

He hadn't been ready to love her.

He was ready now.

He'd hurt her, he knew.

He didn't deserve her forgiveness.

He didn't deserve her love.

But he hoped she'd seen him. That Léon had shown her. That she understood what today meant. That she realised their son... Isaak...and Poppy, they had changed him. Going forward—

He stumbled. The revolving doors to the outside were just there. A few more steps, and his journey going forward would be different. He would be alone. *Again.* But everything was changed now, he knew.

He could never go back to being the man he'd been. Either man. His father's son or the man he'd created to counter it. His DNA.

He'd just be whatever this was. Whoever he was. He would just be it. A man who...*felt*. A man who allowed himself to feel. And right now, he felt hollowed out. He knew what would fill the void. He knew it would only be her. It was only ever *her*. But he knew he couldn't fix what he'd done.

It was out of his control now.

Life, it always had been.

He was not a god.

He was not the devil.

Konstantinos pushed through the revolving doors.

Cameras flashed in his face.

Security surrounded him, and led him through the throng to his waiting car.

His gaze drifted over the journalists being pushed behind a barrier—

He stopped dead. Statue-still.

She was…*here.* In grey sweats, her hair in a loose pony-tail…

'Poppy,' he breathed.

She was being pushed back with the others as if she were no one to him. As if she weren't his—

His heart dropped to his stomach.

She wasn't his wife any more.

He could keep walking, couldn't he? He could look away from her too round, too blue eyes. He could walk away and pretend it did not hurt to see her there. That it did not pain him she stood so far away when his arms ached to hold her.

Or, he could be honest.

He could show her he was human.

He was just a man.

He pushed free of the guards. Step by step, he made his way to her. Stood in front of her.

His insides screamed he was still too far.

'I'm sorry,' he husked as the crowds fell away, and it was just her. Her big blue eyes looking up at him. 'I'm sorry I hurt you, Poppy. I'm—'

'We should go inside. The cameras,' she said, as if it was urgent, as if this moment was not what he wanted the world to see.

He didn't care.

'Let them see,' he said. 'Let them all know I love my…my wife.'

'We're not married any more,' she said quietly.

'I am glad we are not.'

She flinched.

'It is over. The past. But I want to learn from it. I… Forgive me, Poppy,' he demanded because he knew it was what he needed now.

Her forgiveness.

Her love.

'If we could try again,' he continued too quickly—*too breathlessly.* 'A fresh start. A *real* one this time. We could get married again, Poppy. We could start again. Have a family. I want a family with you.' His heart pumped. So hard. *So fast.*

'I love you.'

Poppy started to cry.

She hid her face behind her hands.

Arms came around her. Big and strong.

'Oh, Konstantinos.'

'Everything is going to be okay, Poppy.'

She buried her face into his chest. Into the solidity of him. And she sobbed.

Konstantinos was her safe place.

He was telling her it was okay.

Everything would be okay.

And she believed him.

She lifted her face and he looked down into hers. Poppy raised her hands on his shoulders, raised herself on her tiptoes.

'I love you,' she said, and she kissed him.

They kissed each other.

Not for the camera.

Not for those watching.

They kissed for the only people who mattered.

Them.

EPILOGUE

Three Years Later...

BAREFOOTED, KONSTANTINOS PUSHED his feet into the sand. One step after the other, he walked towards them. His family. Ignorant to his presence, they paddled in the water. Two pairs of tiny legs, twenty tiny wet toes, danced with the sea. Arms waving, they ran away as it came to greet them. Chased it when it receded.

He didn't hurry. He knew they were safe. His daughters. Their hair as black as his, and their eyes as blue as their mother's. He knew their mother watched them. He knew their adoptive grandfather watched them too from his perch on the terrace. Alongside the nannies who hovered higher up the beach, waiting for when they were needed. He knew they were cared for even when he wasn't here.

He knew they were loved.

And Konstantinos loved them all.

'Daddy!'

He bent down low and opened his arms. His daughter ran to him, quickly followed by her twin. He scooped them both up in his arms, and kissed their plump, soft cheeks.

His wife didn't run to him. Too swollen now to run, she waited for him where the sea met the sand. Her belly round beneath her sky-blue dress, wet and hanging heavy at her ankles, she waited for him.

He set the twins down at her feet and, squealing, they ran back to play.

He wrapped his arms around her.

'You're home,' she said. And he knew he was.

The island had lived up to its name. He had found his salvation. Sotiría had become home for them all. For his family. For Léon, who now lived with them. He was family too, a father to both him and Poppy, a grandfather to his children.

'I am,' he said, and pulled her closer. Breathed her in.

She was his air.

His best friend.

Honesty *was* power. The publicity after the talk show had driven his business stocks to never seen before heights. People, it seemed, resonated with second chances. To the rawness of uninhibited love.

And it was raw.

It was beautiful.

And Poppy had given it to him.

The ability to open himself to the possibility of it.

Now he had everything.

They did.

* * * * *

Did you fall head over heels for Broken Greek Vows?
Then don't miss these other dazzling stories by
Lela May Wight!

His Desert Bride by Demand
Bound by a Sicilian Secret
The King She Shouldn't Crave
Italian Wife Wanted
Kidnapped for Her Secret

Available now!

Get up to 4 Free Books!

We'll send you 2 free books from each series you try
PLUS a free Mystery Gift.

Both the **Harlequin Presents** and **Harlequin Medical Romance** series feature exciting stories of passion and drama.

YES! Please send me 2 FREE novels from Harlequin Presents or Harlequin Medical Romance and my FREE gift (gift is worth about $10 retail). I may cancel anytime by emailing ReaderServiceInfo@Harlequin.com or by calling 1-800-873-8635.If I don't cancel, I will receive 6 brand-new larger-print novels every month and be billed just $7.19 each in the U.S., or $7.99 each in Canada, or 4 brand-new Harlequin Medical Romance Larger-Print books every month and be billed just $7.19 each in the U.S. or $7.99 each in Canada. That's a savings of 20% off the cover price! It's quite a bargain! Shipping and handling is just 75¢ per book in the U.S. and $1.75 per book in Canada.* I understand that accepting the free books and gift places me under no obligation to buy anything—they are mine to keep for free no matter what I decide.

Choose one:

☐ **Harlequin Presents Larger-Print**
(176/376 BPA G3CD)

☐ **Harlequin Medical Romance**
(171/371 BPA G3CD)

☐ **Or Try Both!**
(176/376 & 171/371 BPA G3CE)

Name (please print)

Address   Apt. #

City   State/Province   Zip/Postal Code

Email: Please check this box ☐ if you would like to receive newsletters and promotional emails from Harlequin Enterprises ULC and its affiliates. You can unsubscribe anytime.

Mail to the **Harlequin Reader Service:**

IN U.S.A.: P.O. Box 1341, Buffalo, NY 14240-8531

IN CANADA: P.O. Box 603, Fort Erie, Ontario L2A 5X3

Want to explore our other series or interested in ebooks? Visit www.ReaderService.com or call 1-800-873-8635.

*Terms and prices subject to change without notice. Prices do not include sales taxes, which will be charged (if applicable) based on your state or country of residence. Canadian residents will be charged applicable taxes. Offer not valid in Quebec. This offer is limited to one order per household. Books received may not be as shown. Not valid for current subscribers to the Harlequin Presents or Harlequin Medical Romance series. All orders subject to approval. Credit or debit balances in a customer's account(s) may be offset by any other outstanding balance owed by or to the customer. Please allow 4 to 6 weeks for delivery. Offer available while quantities last.

Your Privacy — Your information is being collected by Harlequin Enterprises ULC, operating as Harlequin Reader Service. For a complete summary of the information we collect, how we use this information and to whom it is disclosed, please visit our privacy notice located at https://corporate.harlequin.com/privacy-notice. Notice to California Residents—Under California law, you have specific rights to control and access your data. For more information on these rights and how to exercise them, visit https://corporate.harlequin.com/california-privacy. For additional information for residents of other U.S. states that provide their residents with certain rights with respect to personal data, visit https://corporate.harlequin.com/other-state-residents-privacy-rights.

HPHM2603